M

C

Mag ... hundred square miles of supercity – and last outpost of a civilization devastated by nuclear war
Magellan, home of 50 million human beings enjoying unlimited technical power, material affluence and personal freedom – 50 million sick and lonely people, oppressed by the futility of their existence
Magellan, poised on the eve of 'Liberation', a computer-created paradise of the mind – and a stalking-ground of unimagined terrors

"His demon worlds really reek of terror" – *Evening Despatch*

"A striking Exercise in high fantasy" – *Daily Telegraph*

Magellan

COLIN ANDERSON

SPHERE BOOKS LIMITED
30/32 Gray's Inn Road, WC1X 8JL

First published in Great Britain in 1970 by Victor Gollancz

First Sphere Books edition 1971

TRADE
MARK

Set in Linotype Georgian

Printed in Great Britain by
Hazell Watson & Viney Ltd,
Aylesbury, Bucks

EURI RAN TOWARDS Magellan, along the rusting, iron-railed inspectionway that dangled above the underground river. His mind outran his body—he was terrified that, like the man he'd just killed, he too would part company with his stumbling body. He halted before he lost all control and took a deep breath of the damp, unfiltered air. His footsteps had woken the ghosts that waited and whispered in the tunnel. They gathered just beyond the radius of his light.

The inspectionway trembled and flakes of rust pattered on to the surface of the water a few feet below. Euri shone his light downwards and saw the river skulking past him like a stray cat through its concrete alley, indifferent to him and the ghosts.

He held his breath. Silence spread from him. The little universe that held him waited to see how he would escape it.

Liberation! Liberation!

His breath, a long white streamer, was rapidly frayed as the tunnel caught eagerly at his soul-ghost. The cold crept deeper into his bones. He turned the dial of his suit to FULL but the small battery had not been designed for such an extreme. It was difficult to believe that the weakness lay in himself, the feeble warmth all that his body could produce. He swore at the suit battery, at the quality of his energy pills. He could not stop shaking although he had been running for only a few minutes. He drew his spangled cloak closer about him.

He could hear the ghost of the dead man drawing nearer. It wanted Euri's body for itself.

He had never been told that the dead were like this. The old were long gone from daily life before news came of their passing, had long ceased to make any demands of the living. But the man he'd killed was still young. Euri had left his body twenty minutes ago in the Casino not half a mile away but he could still see that face and knew that he was followed by a powerful adversary—a man who had escaped the body. Those smiling lips! That pallor! Now he knew why grey was evil.

The Gamblers had acted so quickly. When Euri's ball had smashed his opponent's forehead, and the body had fallen to the floor like a vehicle the pilot has abandoned, the spectators had been dispersed and Euri himself, silent and not yet afraid, escorted to the tunnel entrance. By now the Gamblers would all be gone, the dust they'd disturbed replaced and nothing to be seen but a decaying, empty hall which no one had entered for a hundred years. The body would have been disposed of and not even the dead man would ever be able to find it again.

He started to run but stopped, gasping, fearful of the noise he'd made, listening for what he would never hear again, the voice of the dead man.

He ran towards Magellan and this time didn't slow down, despite aching legs and burning throat and the inspectionway which swayed wildly as he ran, until he felt again the rhythm of the city's countless engines, the familiar pulse of its heart. The river was now joined by subsidiary channels, each with its special voice that told what part of the city it came from, and the current swelled and grew faster. The inspectionway here was of newer construction and his footsteps no longer shook it. He slowed to a walk, breathing deeply the breeze that accompanied the channel. His instinct told him when he was close to electronic devices and the ghosts, who could not face the robot surveillance of Magellan, dropped behind.

He found the ladder that led to the inspection hatch and climbed rapidly up it, feet and hands slipping on the narrow rungs. He closed and locked the hatch behind him and lay down in the corridor to rest and think. Above him was a natural window through which there came a thin light. He checked his chronometer and saw that it was morning—the morning of the Last Day. There was little time left if he wanted help.

His deepest instinct told him to find the nearest Emergency Alarm and demand medical alleviation of his fear and its jumble of undesirable emotive by-products; to present his Servant with an even more original and prestigious neurosis. His nerves cried out to be tranquillized, his emotions to be calmed.

The difficulty was that to do so would be to reveal the existence of the Casino which had been kept secret until now. His Servant could do nothing now and the Gamblers themselves, like everyone in the world, would be winding up their activities today. But the full treatment of his fear involved the necessary explanation to him of its roots and he was reluctant to have Death explained. In such an extraordinary case as this the Semantics Academy would send a top man—perhaps a grëat Semantico, as his father had been—to insemanticize his experience and ensure that not the least memory of what he had been through failed to confirm a rationally happy view of life. Now that he was out of the tunnel Euri was conscious of a sense of exhilaration, of vast, shadowed mysteries that made explanations irrelevant. He remembered the promises he had made to the Gamblers and those they had made to him. They had kept theirs—to give life meaning—and he would keep his of secrecy.

He jumped to his feet. The corridor led to a maintenance station that lay on the border between the Old City and the new city of Magellan. The station was only manned by robots of the most elementary intelligence and he easily eluded them. Even without his chronometer he could have told it was morning. The city never looked so unreal, so like a 3-D projection as it did in the morning.

He looked up to where the sky hid the tops of the towers. The soft whiteness and the suggestion of a cool breeze told him it was snowing up there. From the upper floors it would be possible to see the snowflakes but the heat of the city evaporated snow or rain long before it reached ground level. He knew that a white sky meant snow; a grey sky meant rain and a sticky heat; a blue sky brought the odours of the hydroponic farms that covered the hundred square miles of world that lay outside the city and sometimes, fleetingly, the sour, raw smell of the wilderness. When Magellan blazed with light and building reflected building blindingly and the city came completely to life—then it was night.

But *this* night—tonight at Midnight—Liberation would come: the towers die dark and cold, choke in their waste gases, arteries clog and power no longer channelled find release in a thousand violences. Gyroscopically stabilized, electrically braced, pressurized, aerodynamically shaped—what courses would the towers follow, the swiftest path to death?

Death again! To achieve the immortality that Liberation promised could he afford to retain the idea of Death? How stupid to go back into the Old City to search for Death when Magellan promised eternal life, light and power.

Well, tonight all questions would be answered.

Elated, his thoughts stilled in awe of the infinite future that lay ahead of him, he stepped on to the canal and surrendered himself to its current. It was impossible to stop and think once he was in Magellan: the canals—billions of platelets floating on a dense liquid—never paused. The canals flowed in and out of the buildings—which were also pumping-stations—so that Magellan was like a new Venice. Euri studied the streaks of black and yellow that showed where the current was flowing and walked across the spongy surface of the canal until he found himself shooting through the narrow channels between the warehouses and factories that surrounded Magellan. In the centre the current moved swiftly; at the edges it slowed and eddied until it was sucked into the entrance of a building. The air was full of the hiss of the shuffling platelets. From the factories—walls gaudy with the efforts of the thousand winners of this month's Industrial Art awards—came the hum, the rhythm of Magellan, the sound of home. Euri moved from canal to canal until he reached a fast main street that swept him towards the central towers where his apartment was and where he hoped to find his wife.

Few citizens of Magellan cared for the unreal morning hours and there were more animals on some canals than people: ostriches, deer, wolves and tigers rendered amiable by neuro-surgery, were moving in age-old patterns towards the feeding-stations. A group of small deer scattered in bursts before Euri's solitary approach.

What would happen to them after Midnight? What would they make of Eternity?—if they survived. He was not sure if real animals would need to be kept in existence when a man could conjure up one from his thoughts—and more magnificent creatures than tigers! Brighter of eye, faster, stronger, more harmonious than these shabby creatures that slouched towards mealtime. Euri's aesthetic impulses tingled as he thought of the animals he would create when the Brain, his ultimate Servant, made him omnipotent.

To Euri it seemed the city's pulse beat faster this last morning. He felt acutely conspicuous, uneasily conscious of the thousand electronic wave-patterns unstabilized by his unusual appearance at this hour, circuits that strove always to return to a norm. Usually he left the Casino at a time when his appearance amongst the thousands of people on the streets would be such that the robots would not notice it. The unexpected killing had upset his plans. Even now some concerned machine might be alerting the welfare agencies to his abnormal change of habit. He remembered what a machine had once told him: *Liberty is in thinking like everyone else.* Now, oppressed by his secret, he saw the machine's point.

Near Congress Plaza thousands of spider-robots crawled over the towers, spinning the decorations for the last New Year's Eve the city and the world would know. The towers were becoming gigantic flower stems from which blossomed iridescent blooms a hundred yards across, fanfares of neonlight which turned the opaque sky into candy-floss, exploding every minute a million silky seeds ever the startled herds and the artists who were supervising the operations.

On islands in the canal huge glass trees glowed into life —colossal human heads which Euri hardly had time to recognize before they dissolved and became someone else. The Universal Society had so many heroes. He respectfully remarked a family that had been chosen Most Unfortunate Family of the Year; medicos who had identified unsuspected ailments. Once he thought he saw his own face in a series of great medical case-histories and he hurried angrily on. Past working models of the city's sewerage system that he did not dare look at too closely in case he should see himself in miniature running through the tunnel; model hydroponic farms; atomic powerplants; relief maps of the world—a flat world necessarily and not the globe the ancients had known, for that was 99% wilderness and unknown to modern man. Magellan, like a new Jerusalem, lay at the centre of the hundred square miles that was now all the world.

The world was surrounded by forests, bramble-jungles, swamps and grasslands where flourished the sophisticated growths that had sprung up and survived after the radioactivity and poisons of the War had killed the crops. Now, although the effects of the War were long vanished, these new growths were so strong and resistant that they could only be cleared by atomic blasting and the ground gained only held by unremitting and expensive work. The occasional long distance flier that reconnoitred beyond the world returned with pictures of silent wastes; angry, senseless waters.

Euri's return home was delayed by the preparations, but this didn't annoy him: he realized that he was reluctant to face Chrys.

How the robots worked when there were no humans to slow them down! They could never understand the reluctance of humans to drink energy, let it flow through them and put out their full strength. It was necessary to keep a tight control on the robots' activities or they would have been speeding men faster and faster through their life-cycles in order to increase production of the canned corpses in the memorial vaults.

By now there were a few artists on the canal, come to experience the witching hour of morn and dictate poems into their recorders. The last day of the old world, Magellan, the Universal Society! What celebrations there would be—for who would mourn a society that in fulfilling only 99% of its promises had been the most disappointing in history? He became aware that a dozen TV cameras were directed at him and realized that he must have foolishly allowed himself to present an evocative picture as he hurried on, head bent in thought. To how many of those who were responsible for his happiness was the TV showing him?

There was no particular necessity to go home. Like everyone else in a congested city where it would have been ridiculous for millions of people to clog the canals in pursuit of such trivialities, he ate and slept wherever he happened to be. But he needed to know how matters stood between himself and Chrys before he went to work. He eventually reached the foot of his apartment-tower and stepped into a gondola that crawled swiftly up the side of the building—as much for privacy as for economy there were no interior stairs or corridors—wondering if the TV had told his wife of his coming.

He stepped on to his balcony and saw through the glass wall that Chrys was up. The gondola sensed his indecision and waited but he gestured it away and it slid downwards. Even so he found it difficult to enter. Chrys had not turned round. Wild, sweet and natural, at a third pole from good or mistaken as the Universal Society understood it, how neurotic and atavistic she looked! No wonder she had been permitted to bear a child: she must have greatly puzzled the Servants for them to have felt that such a cure for her emotional problems was justified.

Still she refused to acknowledge his presence outside the window and he repeated to himself the advice he'd been given during his briefings as her future paternal emotive-object: to look upon emotional ambivalence—even *hate*—as a normal and even a healthy sign. But he had never been able to take any interest in the coming child.

How lucky he was to be even this much a father he, of course, understood. Only those whom nothing but shock-therapy would cure were permitted the rational parenthoods of overcrowded Magellan. It was illogical to hate the Unknown Parents whose chromosomes, mixed to the correct recipe, were the ingredients of the child Chrys was carrying. Neither she nor he were normal enough to pass on their characteristics. A thousand sessions with his Servant had never succeeded in satisfying his complaints. Now that it was certain that the boy would be born in Eternity he was even more worried what the effect would be on Chrys and himself. Sometimes he believed that the child would somehow become genuinely theirs. At other times he saw it as an unscalable barrier between them, growing and growing without end, for what limits would a child born in Eternity ever know?

How was he to get an answer in the few hours left to him? Did all the world await Liberation in such doubt? He never knew what his healthy inferiors thought. His had been an exceptionally favoured childhood and he had never had much contact with ordinary children.

His mother had been too soon recommended maternal fulfilment by her Servant who had illegally taken advantage of his position to become Euri's father. No wonder Euri was unstable, abnormal, full of weaknesses and undesirable features, so unusual in appearance despite his conventionally expensive face that people turned back to look at him on the canals, puzzled. The product of no more than two parents, half-created from the haphazard conjunction of only two germ-cells, it was a miracle he'd survived. His appearance must have been a great shock to his mother. She had had her innocence, physical and mental, restored shortly after his birth and he'd never known her.

His father had relapsed from his cure and compounded his crime by visiting Euri in his fosterhome and making himself known to the helpless six-year-old. With an egotism so admirably healthy that it had nearly wrecked his case, Euri had immediately rejected both his father and his fosterparents and applied for Deprived Child Status. The complex nature of the case, the unusual feature of his having an actual identifiable paternal emotive object to reject, had ensured him a 100% DCS and his later emotional discomfort over his conduct towards his fosterparents (although they had soon had another and more attractive child to compensate them) had guaranteed him permanent status.

He was as free as any king in the History he specialized in. Others, less talented in misery than himself, gladly undertook his neuroses and lay awake at night with them. He had a Servant to himself who assured him that every second of his unhappy existence imposed a fresh debt on society. When Euri had been unable to think of new demands his Servant had formulated them for him from his wider experience of similar cases. How happy he had been!

Yet he hungered now, and had hungered ever since it had been announced, for Liberation. Strange how quickly his sense of freedom had eroded. He remembered the thrill he'd felt when the DCS papers came and all those he'd known were forever barred from seeing him and poisoning his mind with memories of injustice. In fact his memories of the period before he had gained his distinction were so vague that he concluded—since he believed himself to be a niceguy—that a dangerous excess of feeling had caused his Servant to damp down his emotions with drugs.

In his adolescence he had been proud when strangers asked for his autograph. He had never tired of giving interviews to authors and had watched every TV drama based on his life until they ceased to make him cry.

From time to time he ran across his father in the waiting-rooms of the Medical Academy. He also had done well and was engaged with a large team on the study of the father-son relationship. As a former Semantico he had been easily convinced that the son he had sought had no connection with the actual fact of Euri. It was a long time since Euri had associated him with the thrilling monster that he and his Servant called Father.

Euri felt old. The Press Academy had gone so far as to hint that his life-drama was not living up to expectation. They would love the Casino, the romantic Gamblers and the drama of the killing. If he could have been granted immunity from explanation he would gladly have revealed all, but the creed of the Universal Society ran: To explain all is to forgive all. The Servant of those early days had retired and the young women analysts brought in to exercise his sexual appetite had gone on to better things in Public Health. And gone with them all was that first exhilaration of freedom. If Liberation were to be that exhilaration—a billion-year rapture!

He thought regretfully of the analysts of his youth as he nodded to the TV to let him in. It was some consolation to know that not even the Press Academy had been able to get any more co-operation from his wife than he had himself.

Chrys greeted him: "Did you sleep well?" and in her customary preoccupied way she dialled some food. He looked round the apartment which he had not seen for two or three days. He and Chrys ate out for the most part, slept out in individual sound-proofed cubicles, and made love in 'honeymoon hotels' where every detail of their honeymoon could be reconstructed and lived over and over again. In the apartment they entertained, were photographed, held interviews and were polled. Apartments were showcases where a man could unfold his soul before the public eye without getting in anyone's way. Chrys, who was a sculptor, used theirs as a workshop. It was unimaginative and tasteless. It had recently featured in a hundred articles and TV shows as the epitome of alienation and chic freedom. Even so it seemed peculiarly uncomfortable today. He turned to Chrys and said angrily: "What have you done with your sculptures?"

"Told them to go and cut their little throats."

"At Midnight we'll be liberated! We'll be in Eternity! Why destroy things you've worked on all your life? What will you have to show for your life?"

Chrys didn't answer. Euri was thinking only of himself. He sat down in his personalized armchair but even that rejected him today and he got up and walked agitatedly round the apartment. There wasn't a thing left.

"You've had a busy morning!" he said in wonder.

"A busy night. I've been calling every gallery in Magellan and telling my sculptures to dispose of themselves."

"You can't commit aesthetic suicide! You've forgotten the photos and plans of all your works in the National Archives."

"I know. I was only making a gesture. What else can one do in this world? When I'm omnipotent I shall be able to make genuine destructions.'

A sudden thought sent Euri to his desk. Fortunately his tapes, notebooks, poetry and prose, operas, oratorios, scenarios, the autobiography he'd been working on since he was seven, were all still there.

Chrys laughed: "You don't need all that now. You yourself told me it wouldn't be necessary to understand oneself in Eternity."

"But we shall still need to *communicate*," said Euri.

"If you spent more time listening to *me*—my simple, obvious words—and less time trying to spy on my soul through my immortal works of Art you might know me better. We can forget Art. We have the child to prepare for. He'll be one of the first to be born in Eternity. *Now*, he's simply part of our cure according to the Servants: a new work of Art for me; a new character in your famous life-drama. In Eternity he'll be himself, unique."

"That many-fathered bastard!"

"No more so than your Servant-inspired writings or my Creative Fulfilment works; my Anonymous, Classical, Folkloristic works of Art! If you only knew how much I've hated Art—the record of my mistakes, my failures, my weaknesses."

"You're disillusioned by this finite world. Eternity will be like the works of Art you've dreamed of and could never create."

"I thought the purpose of immortality was more *life*?"

Euri was silent, remembering the sullen, ugly artefacts fitted with elementary brains that had shambled round the apartment, impressing even the TV with their air of unsatisfied, savage cravings. After all, he wasn't sorry to see them gone.

"I never knew you felt like this," he said at last. "I wonder why my Servant never told me? Of course I've been so exceptionally busy these past months. Under normal circumstances our marriage would have occupied my entire time and most of that of our Servants. By now we could have hoped to have some small understanding of each other. Chronophage developed so unexpectedly fast that we've had to work day and night to make sure that it would be adequately informed before going into operation. All of the Academies have been working at top priority on Chronophage's education, and History has been the most important field."

"These things haven't made us happy up till now."

"We've never had the time to assimilate and co-ordinate all our knowledge, nor the power to use even what little knowledge we had. But Chronophage's resources are almost infinite. With its help we'll be omnipotent—at least on the surface of the Earth—and as immortal as the Sun. Even when the Sun expires in a billion years' time Chronophage will have had ample time to discover new sources of energy. We can't conceive any limit to the eventual powers of Chronophage. It's a million times larger than any brain we've yet built. We have Eternity ahead of us to find our happiness."

"Midnight tonight! I can't believe it. Eternity! It seems to me the world *ends* at Midnight. I shan't want to live this life for a billion years."

"That's only your weak, time-bound spirit talking. When you have unlimited strength you will need Eternity to work in. We live for as long as we have work to do. There'll be no growing old for us."

She didn't reply. She looked past him, through the glass wall, to where the sky was lifting from the towers of Magellan. No one ever escaped him so completely as Chrys was capable of doing. He knew no way of bringing her back. Why hadn't he taken a greater interest in Communications as a child? He said nothing: the TV was listening and the last thing he wanted to suggest was that the therapy of which Chrys formed an essential part was not succeeding. At this moment Eternity seemed to him like an ocean with only scattered happy islands that could easily be missed in its immensity. Their marriage was less than a year old but now he couldn't imagine life without her. Yet there was nothing in his life he felt less sure of—Eternity without her would seem long indeed.

He hadn't told her about his killing. Shouldn't he tell her before they entered Eternity? But he remembered his extraordinary fear in the tunnel: he didn't want the dead man to pursue Chrys also into Eternity. He decided to shelve the problem for the time being. It was time he made an appearance at the History Academy. There, where he was accustomed to manipulating intractable facts and where his Servant was also Director, he would be able to think more rationally. He said: "I'll come back to take you to the Office Party."

"No. I have a lot to do. I have to see my Servant to explain why I've relinquished my Art Grant and after that I have to see my Ante-natal Board—you may catch it on TV. I'll see you at the Academy."

"Very well. Fourth watch after Noon."

She went to lie down on the divan in the other room and before she dimmed the lights he saw that she had spared at least one of her works, his favourite picture, a dream landscape she had painted shortly after they were married. It showed a country where Nature flowered peacefully under a cloudless sky; a country where peace did not mean death. He wondered if they would reach that land after Liberation. It looked remote—at the very end of Eternity. He put the thought out of mind.

He was tired and he had a busy day ahead. From his medipack he selected a white pill to keep him awake, a grey pill to set his mind at rest, a red pill to give him energy and a yellow pill to make him happy. When he was omnipotent he would need no such artificial aids.

He ate the breakfast because Chrys had dialled it, but he was not hungry. He washed and perfumed himself and dressed again in the cloak he'd worn at the Casino. It was spangled with red and blue crosses, crescents and stars, hammers and sickles, pentagons: all images of ancient magic—yet they had failed to protect him from killing.

His face in the TV was as aloof as ever. It didn't know

Euri and didn't want to. Why had his father ordered him such an expensive face? And had the bad taste to have it modelled after his own arrogant features? It must have looked as coldly back at him as it now did at Euri. He stared long and hard at himself and in response the TV, a simple soul, formed his name for him in gold letters: Euripides Che Fourthojuly 1070121.

He laughed: who would remind him in Eternity?

He checked his chronometer. The tenth watch before Noon. Day 365. Year 2079. He put it to his ear and listened to the tiny electric voice which repeated over and over for Euri and itself: *Om mani padme h'mmmmm. . . .*

Out on the balcony Euri found the sun now slanting steeply down through the steel and glass forest of Magellan. In a circle round the city, held back by the cannon of the Meteorological Army, snowclouds were banked up like a huge arena. He approved. He was glad that others knew how wrong it would be to enter Eternity under those clouds. He called for the gondola and descended to street level.

Unsung Heroes Street was full of pedestrians and low-scudding fliers. Disturbed by the tension, the animals were padding or galloping through the streets, sniffing the air, herding together and avoiding humans, sending showers of platelets flying as they fled over the canal. Euri hurried towards Congress Plaza. His appearance was attracting more looks than ever—half contempt, half envy. He was surprised by the familiarity of some of these glances, but of course it was impossible to know if he knew any of those watching him. People changed their faces every week. Some would have changed their sex. Some, on the advice of their medicos, would have escaped to a new life by undergoing a personality-change. Some, never sleeping and living on drugs, would have been ageing twice as fast as Euri and now be years older. Euri himself kept to the youngest age permitted for his birth-group: the world was so crowded that no one could be allowed to occupy space for a longer time than the average.

There were as yet no infants in vehicles come in groups for the sights and no unescorted children—in these days of rationed pregnancies there were too many attempted kidnappings. He passed licensed gangs of teen-agers and solitary old men, women in groups and young couples, but no one looked confident or happy except the delegations of pre-teens who marched along with implacable dignity. At the age of ten after an intensive education the child became officially adult. He took his rights and his civic duties seriously. At that age, after a perfectly regulated childhood, he was neurosis-sterile. He had no sex problems: sex was nothing but a pleasure. He was an enthusiastic reformist conservative. Most social reforms were pushed through by ten-year-olds. They were the backbone of the Universal Society. Later came the inevitable wear and tear of heart and mind and the rest of life became a battle against mental discomfort. Euri swallowed two more happiness pills, determined to shake off his . . . fear . . . yes, *fear*. The second attack within twenty-four hours. He would have to have it seen to.

In Congress Plaza, the enormous mushroom dome of Congress—symbol of the Universal Society in aluminium. The mushroom represented power over Nature in the form of atomic energy; power over the mind in the form of hallucinogenic drugs. It represented the umbrella of the Constitution that sheltered all citizens equally. On the red flag the white mushroom could also look like a tree of life or an arrow pointing heavenwards. To Euri it had always seemed to be an eyeless skull.

His destination was the History Academy which, along with the Academies of Art, Psychology, Medicine, Semantics, Science and the Press, overlooked Congress. Before going to his office, however, he paused at the foot of the great statue of Magellan the Explorer, which crouched in ancient costume of 'top hat and tails' with the globe of the Earth on his shoulders, eyes searchlights that illuminated the entrance to Congress. An inscription revolving round the base said in coloured lights: *Magellan—the First Man to Circumnavigate the Globe and Prove that All Folks is Neighbours.* On impulse, Euri decided to attend Congress on this last day.

He entered the dome along with several hundred others and experienced the familiar sensation of dwindling to midget size beneath its giant proportions. Far beneath him in the central arena the main proceedings were taking place. He found a free desk and the TV rapidly recapitulated the day's business for him. Nothing extraordinary had been revealed. Questions about the nature of Eternity, the functioning of Chronophage, the winding-up of the Universal Society, were receiving the same answers that they had received for the past year. The issues were honours awards and Euri voted a blanket *Yes* to show goodwill. A man with as many public distinctions as he had could afford to be generous. He toyed with the microphone, wondering whether to make a farewell speech. No one except his Servant would ever take the trouble to listen to it but he liked to make a demonstration of his rights from time to time. It pleased him to think that his words, translated into the thousand dead languages, would be preserved for all time in the Archives. Moreover, it occurred to him that his Servant would have no more opportunity to harm him and he could pour out his hatred of the world he lived in and his longing for Eternity and freedom.

At that moment the TV thought to inform him that all speeches were now being directly relayed to Chronophage. He put the microphone down, reluctant to leave a valedictory impression in the memory of the great brain that was to give him eternal life.

From Congress he went directly to the History Academy, a 300-storey monument to Man the Voyager, chequered in the traditional 'window-pattern'. Every style of architecture since the dawn of civilization had been incorporated in the structure and consequently it had just that ramshackle incoherence that Euri and his colleagues strove to eliminate from History. As the canal circled slowly round Congress Plaza towards the History Academy, Euri studied the series of murals, called *The Ascent of Man*, that covered one side of that building. The first of the murals at ground-level showed Early Man who stood—the artist having been unable to imagine what Early Man found to do with his time—round-shouldered and disconsolate. Pre-war history was, in fact, largely speculative. The Great Tribal Atomic War had left the Universal Society an incomparable legacy of scientific knowledge and technical expertise but the libraries, the museums and galleries that were spoken of as existing before the war having been used to shelter the non-combatant population had been utterly destroyed. What little had remained of Art and History was all the more prized. No efforts were spared to increase production of these marks of true civilization.

Another Early Man in a mural higher up had found a round stone and was looking at it with an ambiguous grimace. That stone had led Man into a ten thousand year detour away from Nature. Euri, himself to be an Early Man of the next era, wondered what the round stone of that age would be.

In the mural above that the beginnings of agriculture, houses and walls against prospective enemies. Above that again twin brothers were engaged in battle. The victor had dropped his sword and hid his face in his hands and his victim-brother looked up at him with an expression that the official brochure, in a 30,000 word essay, described as *forgivenessfull* and *ethic-triumphant.*

Next they were building cities, bartering, painting, making music and constructing boats and aircraft. By now the murals had climbed out of sight but Euri knew what came next: the machines that grew from puppets into the monsters that had fought the War over men's heads. The mural that should have shown the War had been left blank as a mark of respect and there had never been a mural of the Universal Society. What could it show?

The Universal Society was dedicated to ensuring that all men were equal. Men *were* equal and if the status they temporarily held was necessarily unequal the robots were there to prevent any man abusing the rights of other men. Machines guaranteed the efficiency and stability of the Universal Society. The mural would have to show a lattice of statuses upheld by machines and men as no more than amoebas struggling to find shape within it.

In Eternity, if it were possible to die, surely a man would leave behind him an eternal void, an unfillable status?

Liberation! Liberation!

After Liberation, what? Once again there would be a man gazing wide-eyed at a world of his own, wide, beautiful and empty. No machines; no walled buildings. No battles—no History!

Tonight! He could not believe it. Eternity must always lie beyond the horizon.

The History Academy, like an anteater, sucked him in between the Stonehenge pillars of its entrance.

There was no sensation of the size and weight of the building. The bright lights came from all directions and there were no shadows: the building could have been made of cardboard. The canal passed through the building. Euri stepped off at the pier leading to his department and saw in front of him the round shoulders and stoop—stigmata of the more heavily burdened statuses—of his Servant, Bubo. The Servant, who was also the Director of the Academy, turned and, seeing Euri, constructed a look of surprised pleasure on his features. Euri, who had had a lifetime of special care, was not fooled. Bubo had been waiting for him.

After a conventional greeting Bubo said: "I'm glad to see you so early. I wanted to ask your permission to visit your computers on this final day. They've been doing a fine job and I've never yet had the pleasure of seeing them."

"Very well."

He didn't trust himself to say more. With luck Bubo might not have heard yet of his strange early morning walk and every minute gained was valuable. There was still plenty of time for Bubo to order a mnemectomy if he discovered the severity of Euri's illness.

Bubo scurried politely at his side with the model manners of a Director to his assistant but Euri knew for whom the lights lit and the doors flew open that millisecond sooner. Machines did not like deviants nor respect the powerless. Silently he led the way to his office, a portable pneumatic working office hanging from the ceiling of the computer hall that was his province. Before the chairs were even inflated the machines demanded his help, and for some time he was too busy to remember Bubo and his problems. When he did have a moment to spare he saw that Bubo was standing at the outward-sloping window and watching the computers with uncomfortable curiosity.

Like all visitors, Bubo's attention had fixed on D47 which grumbled away to itself in annoyance that its old-fashioned tape-feed would go no faster. Poor D47! A machine's machine, with a poor digestion for human data, it had once spewed out and entirely obliterated several years catalogued—if Euri could remember correctly—under the title *World War One*. He had had to work night and day to make a neat repair of the hole in the fabric of History but he was an excellent Historician, and History, after he'd cobbled it together again, was considerably more inspiring, picturesque and even logical than the actuality had appeared to be—which was as it should be.

The computers whirled in rhythmic ecstasy, playing permutations, headlong into infinity. They needed so little: a handful of data a day and they would retire into their dark interiors in introspective rapture. With one fact they could cast a line into the darkness; with two facts they could spin a web to catch a world; with three facts they could *make* a world; and with four, a Universe. Euri hated to stop, to kill them by directing them into some finite pattern. But he knew that he was being sentimental for they had no concept of that void he sailed his ego-ship above, struggling even in dreams to hold to the vessel no matter where it drifted.

"The first time I've seen your department," said Bubo thoughtfully, "and it will be the last, I'm afraid. However, although I know you have an unusual affection for these . . . beings—which I don't condemn for one moment—I myself, as an ordinary individual, I shall be glad when we can communicate with each other and the world without inhuman interpreters interposing.'

"Yet Chronophage itself is nothing but a giant computer."

"Possibly. But Chronophage will enable mind to join mind in direct union. I have no fear of Chronophage. It's not a little machine with a little mind of its own like a robot but a universal channel that will enable our will and intelligence to work directly on the world around us. What progress we shall make when our wishes are perfectly implemented and not perverted by incompetent machines! Infinite progress!"

It irritated Euri to have to agree with him. Bubo, short and fat—Servants were not expected to add beauty to their other advantages—hardly seemed capable of outreaching infinity.

"Does it ever occur to you how little we accord with the dignity of immortality?" he asked.

"How fond you are of these archaisms! What does 'dignity' signify but 'rights'? And rights are simply what we can obtain. We can now obtain immortality and therefore we are worthy of it."

"Has that question ever been put to Chronophage?"

"Of course not. It would have no meaning for a

machine."

Euri could see by the warmth of the other's smile how annoyed he was by this line of thought. So much the better: it would prevent Bubo from turning to more embarrassing topics. He said: "We've put every other question to the Brain—the requests, demands, opinions of every single human being in the world. We've fed it with our accumulated wisdom in History, Psychology and so forth—what we believe we are and what we hope to become. Why don't we ask what *it* thinks before we surrender ourselves to it?"

"Machines *don't* think! You've worked too long with robots. They have no independent judgement. And thank God for that! These machines killed 99 per cent of the human race in the Tribal War. If we believed they *thought* we should have to destroy them."

Bubo's unfortunate reference to the War caused them both discomfort. Yet it had been the birthplace of the Universal Society, that legacy of the one nation that had survived the War due to its advanced technology and development of hydroponic farms that could grow food away from the contaminated land.

Magellan was built on the ruins of the only city of that great nation which had not been completely destroyed, for in the end the cities of the victorious nation, desperate to protect food and medical supplies, had turned their weapons on each other until only one was left, depopulated and demoralized.

That war had at last convinced men of the need to make a true brotherhood, to create a world where no one would ever again have an excuse for turning on his fellow men.

One hundred years after the War this aim was largely achieved but the Universal Society was by its very nature prevented from remaining satisfied with a 99·716 satis-quotient. The last vestiges of prejudice, envy and hatred proved impossible to eradicate and quick to grow again under the wrong conditions. The creation of Chronophage was the result, a computer which would enable every man to be omnipotent, immortal, invincible—the answer to every aim of the Universal Society. No man need be feared. No man need be envied. No man need be depended upon. No man need have less than another. Every man could have exactly what he wanted.

The machines sighed in their depths. Soon they would be needed no longer. Chronophage would do all that they did. From tonight there would be no more History.

Euri was sorrier for the machines than he was for the man he'd killed. He saw once more the Casino in that abandoned museum of space travel where rockets and spaceships even now, rusting and crippled, pointed to the stars. The dead man had, after all, chosen his fate.

"Will Chronophage help us reach the stars?" he asked.

"The stars!"

Bubo smiled coquettishly. He was seriously annoyed. Space was as disturbing a concept as War. "It's well known that Inner Space is larger than Outer Space. There is infinity to be explored within us! We are alive: the Universe is dead. We know this. Most of the Solar System was investigated by robot rockets before the War. Rocket bases were established on the Moon, Mars and one of the moons of Jupiter. All these worlds were barren and the bases could only be maintained at enormous expense. We can only guess at the sums involved since it seems to have been customary in those days to measure expense in terms of Schools. We are told that the money spent on the Mars base alone would have enabled every man, woman and child on Earth to have had two Schools each.

"The bases were destroyed from Earth at a very early stage of the War since it was prohibitively expensive to equip them with the necessary defence systems. Sometimes we get reports of radio messages from them—calls for help and so on—but it's only a kind of claustrophobic hysteria that Eternity will cure. We get a spate of these reports every seven years and there were a lot shortly after the birth of Chronophage was announced. These matters are kept quiet: hysteria is worse than a virus.

"What do we need with a Universe? A greater universe lies within each of us. Why go to Sirius when you can create something a thousand times more amusing?"

But Euri believed that Sirius must have marvels he couldn't begin to imagine and he detested Bubo for exposing his limitations. He turned back to his work and said nothing. Hate was an emotion best cultivated in absence. Bubo was not responsible for his status or what he was.

The newborn babe's first cries were interpreted by an attendant technician: metabolism, heredity, weight; the infant's reactions to hot and cold, soft and hard, vibrations high and low, brightly coloured objects; the pattern of its eye-movements, its leg and arm gestures—all were messages the new personality, uncontaminated by reactions to the actions and ideas of others, transmitted so much more clearly and sincerely than any adult.

As soon as the child could read it was provided with a detailed analysis of itself, a guide to its abilities, desires and needs. Servants watched over every child and saw that every weakness was guarded from hurt and that no frustration dammed vital energies. No little Napoleons brooded in obscurity: they became Sports Instructors or exhausted dreams of empire in the Census Bureau. The luckiest, those whose interests were found to lie in the manual gratifications, graduated to gaily and giddily painted workshops where they performed what the robots could never be made to understand, artistic handicrafts.

The others in varying degree according to their abilities were required to assist in upholding the structure of a society where no pauper escaped education, no sickness escaped cure, where the curiosity of the child in the sandbox was stimulated and satisfied, the sexual awakening of the adolescent in the Youth Centre properly directed, where maturity was fulfilled in responsibility and the complaints of the Senior Citizen encouraged and collected right up to the day, forecast by the medicos, of the final sleeping pill.

Those whose duty it would be to Serve were filtered through intelligence tests, loyalty tests, motivation tests, tests for any taint of racial incest, tests by every sect of psychology, sanity tests, insanity tests, tests to test reactions to being tested. School records, voting records from the age of five were analysed.

There emerged from this ordeal a handful of men whose records, open to public inspection, showed them to be in every respect the ideal. Their ideas, feelings and beliefs were demonstrated to be humane, just, modest—in short *right*—by every known system of morality. For his labours and his endurance of the natural contempt of the other grades for his shameful duties the Servant had one solace: he knew he was infallible.

Bubo's shoulders as he watched the machines were more

hunched than ever; Euri was reminded of the statue of Magellan. He continued his work uncomfortably although there was little left for him to do. The computers had finished their main programme some days ago, right on schedule. Euri only had to check that no insignificant historical incident overlooked in setting up the programme had caused the computers to indulge some wild flight of fancy. But all was well. Chronophage was fully and accurately informed of the History of the World and now only the final hours and minutes of the Universal Society remained to trickle into the great brain.

The room trembled slightly as one of the computers switched off. Euri's thoughts were guilty ones—of Chrys, the dead man, the doomed machines and his unhappy career.

"Chronophage must be stirring under our feet," Bubo said, turning lightly and nervously.

In the liquid iron core of the Earth, Chronophage, the Time-Devourer, the greatest Brain of all, was growing at unbelievable speed. It was only a few months ago that engineers had succeeded in drilling through the Earth's crust and injecting into the core the nucleus of the Brain. Chronophage, outpacing all predictions, making use of the tremendous energies existing there, was probing with its tendrils along stress-contours, flowing with magnetic currents, flooding the dark centre of the Earth with awareness.

Euri studied his controls: they reported blankfaced that all was normal and the TV knew nothing. Congress was still in session. It was not far off Noon. The hours before Midnight stretched like a smaller Eternity.

"Shall we be able to control Chronophage after all?" Bubo said as if to himself.

"What's that?" said Euri, startled. "We shall *be* Chronophage. When the engineers close the circuits at Midnight we shall all be united in Chronophage. *We* shall exert those powers. *We* shall make the molecules of earth and air as far as the limits of the Earth's magnetic envelope cohere at our bidding. Chronophage and all our minds will be on the same wavelength. How can we fail to control ourselves? How can we be harmed when the land and sky themselves conform to our desires? We shall be invulnerable, immortal! There'll be no more problems of right and wrong: everything will be right for us. We shall have everything we desire."

He was enraged that Bubo should try to undermine his confidence in Eternity.

"But have you thought what will happen to you when there is nobody able to guide you? I've been your Servant for some time now and I'm ashamed to admit I haven't enabled you to adjust to a relatively simple environment like this. You haven't been happy in Magellan: how do you hope to be happy in Eternity?"

"Eternity will be a simpler environment than this and it's exactly the kind of happiness only possible in Magellan that I want to escape."

"Escape! Always escape! Where are fifty million people to escape to—even in Eternity? What will happen when fifty million dreams collide?"

"Maybe we'll live in the interstices of each other's worlds," Euri said, "like primitive motion pictures where to the people on the screen the movement seems continuous. We'll never know how many other worlds coexist. What will it matter if fifty million dreams collide? The faster our world is destroyed the faster we shall re-create it

—our world will vibrate faster and therefore seem more real to us. There'll be time and enough to spare in Eternity. Some will sleep while others dream. Anyway, the only possible cause of collision in Eternity will be contamination from the Past and isn't that what we've been working to sterilize?"

They could look back on their work with satisfaction. That evil burden of the Past, History—properly understood—blamed, condemned, fixed guilt on no one. Men could enter Eternity without hatred or misconceptions. For years Historicians had studied each 'fact' that had been uncovered in the debris of the ancient world until they found its place on the four-dimensional graph of History which had to be squared until justice was done and every betrayal proven to be unavoidable and therefore blameless.

"I suppose," Bubo said complacently, "a better name for us would have been the Academy of Truth."

He had good reason for his complacency. Eternity had made the primacy of the History Academy clearer. The aims of the Psychology Academy would be meaningless in Eternity where nothing could repress mind or body; those of the Art Academy meaningless when creation was as natural as breathing; those of the Semantics Academy meaningless when the World and Meaning were identical; those of the Science Academy when men were like Gods. Historical Truth alone would retain its importance, a dread inheritance, and Bubo and his staff had succeeded in purifying it, making it logically, scientifically and psychologically respectable.

Euri only wondered why the work had not had its intended therapeutic effect on himself. Searching for the excuse in all human conduct it had been expected that he would have a better resistance to the guilt that he struggled against.

They took their lunch in the office. It was a scantier meal than usual as the chefs were preparing for the Office Party later in the day. Bubo and Euri toasted Eternity and each other in wine, Bubo pursing his lips at the bitterness of the wild-grape champagne Euri favoured, a perverse luxury. Both were immersed in their thoughts and Euri was surprised to discover a distinct sadness in himself, perhaps the after-effects of what he had been through.

After the meal they called in the TV which, with an artistic sweep that Euri could never knock out of it, took them first on a tour of the streets of Magellan to show them the gathering crowds, the growing movement and excitement.

Where were they all going? Liberation would come to them at Midnight wherever they might be.

Euri grunted in annoyance and the TV hurriedly switched to Congress. Today's President was praising the History Academy . . . the foundation stone of the Universal Society, the conscience of the world, the pontoon bridge over the foul seas of propaganda and mistrust . . .. Great conflicts had raged through the ancient world—the Quality *v.* the Quantity; the Proletariat *v.* the Amateuriat; the Overpigmented *v.* the Underpigmented—strange diseases that could never trouble us again. . . .

The lottery winners who won the Presidency never said anything new. Euri snapped his fingers irritably and the TV tried on him the Youth Representative, a five-year-old girl. He could remember when the Youth Representative had been as old as ten but idealism seemed ever more the province of the very young. The little girl was lisping prettily . . . the Universal Society provided security but challenge; equality but incentive; integration with variety; liberty with individual responsibility and occupation-idealism; religious freedom yet tolerance; individualism that found its purpose in national aims. . . .

"I wonder why this damned machine will never accept that I hate this kind of thing?"

"The imperfect vocalization of high ideals. . . ?"

"I mean I hate the ideals," Euri said automatically in his best 100% DCS manner. "I thought the whole idea of Eternity was to make this kind of thing unnecessary? Ideals are only chains to prevent people tearing each other limb from limb. Ideals cripple us in this life. Why are people still clinging to the Universal Society? Give examples," he instructed the TV.

The TV accordingly quoted the case of the Students Union which had insisted on the examination date being advanced (and automatic top marks for all students since they would have no time to prepare) so they should not be hurled statusless into Eternity; the Senior Citizens who had expedited their deaths only days before they were to become immortal; the demand for gold, uranium, postage-stamps, authenticated pre-war art treasures, government guarantees. . . .

"*Government* guarantees! When there'll *be* no more government!"

"It's a gratifying vote of confidence in the essential stability of our system," replied Bubo. "Of course the Universal Society will survive Eternity. Some sort of organization will be needed even there and the Universal Society was designed with paradise in mind."

"It won't survive *my* Eternity. I enter Eternity alone."

"Without wife or family?"

"Close relationships won't be broken."

"Can you be sure? If you abandon the rest of us can you be sure your wife will follow you into the wilderness? I know how attached you are to Chrys. Did you think of this when you voted for Liberation?"

"I only had a fifty-millionth part of that decision. Are you saying you voted against Liberation? Why do you talk as if you had doubts? I know as well as you that Liberation couldn't have been proposed without the approval of the Servants. Are you saying now it was a mistake?"

"The engineers say everything is going to plan."

"Don't you believe them?"

"Engineers are always right," Bubo said. "Chronophage will do everything they predict. No, I have no doubts of Eternity. The ultimate conquest of Nature! When I was a boy it would have been laughed at if it had been suggested in a TV-drama but everything progresses faster and faster. For some people Eternity will be a welcome halt to Progress. Perhaps those Senior Citizens thought it was all nothing but a bad dream, some consequence of growing old, so they decided to put an end to existence. If you had had my training you would appreciate the dangers. You are right: our society is dying. But you can't separate people and society. After all they're one and the same thing. Even your super-individualism is only the result of the special attention we've given you to correct the harm we did you. I wonder what will happen to everyone when the Universal Society dissolves?"

"And Servants are out of a place?"

"That too."

They were startled by an archaic brassy fanfare from

the TV—it was always pestering the history computers for special effects. This time it was to draw their attention to the ceremonies that marked the end of the year—and this year of the Universal Society itself.

Congress was packed. The TV reported that 2,746,991 speeches were being simultaneously recorded. The President announced the order of business and soon from high up under the dome a gondola could be seen descending with the Chief Accountant and his phalanx of advisers.

The Budget: a triumphant year—the Art Appropriation had been the largest ever. No less than 10,714 geniuses, a quarter of a million talents of the first order and seven million youngpromisings had been certified.

"We're still a long way from that great ideal: every man a genius," said Bubo.

The other items of the Budget were unremarkable except for a sharp rise in the Psychology Academy expenses, but that had been expected in view of the advent of Eternity. Atomic power, robots and machines, a stable population in a self-contained world: Magellan ran as steadily as a chronometer. Even the cost of Chronophage proved to be relatively minor. After its seeding into the Earth's core it had grown of its own accord, its education effected through radio messages.

After the Budget the centre of Congress was cleared for the Annual Commemorative Soccer Performance, the greatest ceremony of the year. Euri and Bubo leant forward in their seats and the TV crept closer in excitement.

To thunderous applause the two teams came out on to the green platform: the Light Browns *v.* the Greys. This match by the top-voted composer of the year, who now ran on to the platform to conduct his composition, would express the aspirations of the world.

Euri breathed a prayer: let the match be in a major key. He could not face the nihilistic pessimism that a defeat for the Light Browns would reveal or the soulless disillusion of a 0-0 draw.

With shouts of joyful admiration they viewed a first half that quickly revealed itself to be a witty and graceful 4-4 scherzo. The pirouettes of the backs, the swoops and glides of the forwards, the aerial gymnastics of the goalkeeper, all the complex rhythm of the game controlled by the composer's staccato whistle, the easy, almost artless, flow—sure sign of the highest genius—all this induced an agonizing exhilaration. It was an inspired composition: one of the Light Brown goals was scored from a pyramid of no less than eight players, the centre-forward at the apex heading the ball down past the Grey goalkeeper who was symbolically blinded by the floodlights. The ecstatic dances that followed each goal were also well-conceived and in harmony with the character of the goal.

In the interval Bubo said: "Do you know why the match is in two movements and the teams change ends? I discovered why only the other day. It had always puzzled me as illogical and arbitrary. I learnt that the ancients engraved musical sounds on discs which *had to be turned over halfway through.* From this we derive our simple and effective two-movement pattern, thesis and antithesis, and all its profound philosophical implications."

Euri could say nothing. The reports of the perspiration-readings and encephalographic scanning that measured the audience's enjoyment showed it to be at the highest pitch of emotion. He wondered how Eternity would come. Would Magellan simply vanish? Would his dreams come true on the moment and Midnight become eternal Morning? Or must he destroy the world and create heaven inch by inch? No! Eternity had to be like the Soccer Performance, easy, joyous, flowing, triumphant!

The second movement was a titanic struggle in which the Light Browns were soon two goals down but then a magnificently conceived logic, an invincible counterpoint, demonstrated that the forces of good must always be victorious. The final reconciling goal did not shatter the Grey net, however, until the last second of the match and Bubo fell back into his seat gasping with relief.

"7-6! The Great Major key. Of course! What else could it be?"

As they descended from Euri's office—which collapsed behind them with a sigh—and walked through the hall on their way out the computers wished them a 'Happy Eternity' in place of the usual 'Happy New Year' and then fell silent, retreated from the time-world. They would never work again. They knew—but were they *aware* of it? No doubt they had different concepts of life and death but it was difficult to believe that these intelligent beings were less related to him than the speechless animals that stumbled through the streets, bewildered and timid. He would miss his machines—old, grumbling D47; Sovac, the big computer in the refrigerated room with its cumbersome mental processes and guilty memories of war-games; the bright new micro-computers who followed him round the hall and could never get problems difficult enough to satisfy them. They never whined to be different. They loved their work. He would rather have stayed with them and asked their views on death and Eternity than go to the Office Party.

He had never liked the Annual Office Party, that great love-feast of the Universal Society, but even a 100%DCS didn't excuse him. A direct refusal to participate would have meant his being rushed to a Psychological Observation Ward. Yet he hated meeting people. The mingled pity and envy that his 100%DCS aroused in others infuriated him. There were always some who would come up with well-meant fresh cures for his famous complaint, half-drawing TV cameras from their wallets to capture what they were sure was to be a historic moment, the dawning joy and gratitude on his face. He had had the satisfaction of sending some of them flying for psychological assistance. For Bubo, however, the Party was the peak of the year, the holy orgy, when simple joy reigned. He would speak of the immemorial antiquity of the ceremony, seeing an ideal Past, a primitive frieze where Boss was in eternal pursuit of Typist.

All over the building, offices were closing down. Euri felt in his very bones the silence that remained when the thousand-and-one machines were shut off and the humans, by themselves feeble and cold, joined on the spiralling ramp that carried them to the top of the Academy. A procession of floors unfolded one after the other as the ramp took him past them, each with a million secrets, not secret by design but because of the inability of any one man to assimilate, far less comprehend, them. It gave him a vivid idea of the greatness of Chronophage that could digest all these materials along with those of the other Academies.

Through the glass dome that crowned the History Academy he saw a few early stars in the colourless sky, itself a kind of Eternity, a waste that cast on to the shores of human perception only a handful of stars. Euri hastily turned away. Bubo had left to see to his duties. Chrys had not yet shown up. He looked round the room. His colleagues—what people to enter Eternity with! He couldn't see what kept them alive: puppets of the Universal Society; copies of TV stars; walking examples of out-of-date psychologies; bundles of Servant-inspired wants.

Euri, antisocial, craved release from stimulus. He ordered a 'Night Ride to the Arctic Cap' drug cocktail in a one watch strength and was glad of the icy expanse that rapidly lengthened between himself and the Party. He avoided the main group of people and walked over to the gallery that commanded a view of Congress Plaza and far out over Magellan towards the Old City. He was startled to see the outlying districts dimming even as he watched and Congress Plaza increase in brightness as if Magellan was collapsing in on itself. There must be an enormous inwards movement of the population.

From this elevation he could see the large blot of darkness that was the Old City and its stumps of buildings piercing the misty, distant horizon. To Euri now the dead man and all the scene of his flight from the Casino had that tiny brightness that was the result of the drugs he'd taken. Although he was well aware of this he was still troubled by the *mechanicalness* of the picture. He had thought himself a free agent outside society. In his mind-picture it enacted itself again with all the awful inevitability of a tenth-rate TV drama.

Liberation!

Behind the hilarity and noise of the conversation a hush lay like a velvet backcloth, the mark of a highly expensive Party. There were no robots to be seen. Servants moved through the domed hall serving drinks. The lights were dimmed to allow a hazy moon, rising over the towers of Magellan, to disclose itself. Disguised psychetectives—easily spotted—were already sampling the emotional temperature and two cases of ego-damage had been rushed out on stretchers.

Bubo's laughter rang out here and there through the room and sometimes Euri caught a glimpse of his round, shiny grin. Bubo enjoyed the traditional insults and obscenities hurled at him by those holding less responsible statuses.

Euri was excused from serving by his 100%DCS. He stood with his back to the glass wall staring through the crowd. It seemed to him he could see tendrils forming in the smoky air, expectations of unjustified pleasure, extending from one person to another only to dissolve into nothingness at the moment of apparent achievement, attenuated by the very act of extension. He shook his head to clear it. He hadn't expected this final Party to be like former ones but—was it the drugs or the imminence of Eternity?—these people looked like nightmare glassfish in an aquarium, wriggling and darting at any scrap of food.

A pill soon dissolved this distressing vision and he was glad to see that Chrys had arrived and was standing with Bubo's wife, Leni, a critico from the Press Academy. Both were looking solemn but Leni's face was a wooden mask and Chrys's an aura that vanished as he attempted to penetrate it.

He walked across the room to greet them. Leni had had a face-change but her new, perfect features still expressed the same triumphant lechery. Criticos were the nearest thing to the ancient priesthood that Magellan had. Like prophets they could not be appointed to the profession: it was a vocation. They were the people's voice when it demanded referendums, demo-guardians, corruption-destroyers. They had power to go where they pleased, access to any place at any time. No official could refuse their questions. Euri himself continually suffered from them on the two counts of holding high status at the History Academy, and thus a potential public enemy, and as 100%DCS an object of public sympathy. Leni had taken a special interest in him. She treated him with a mixture of contempt for the helplessness of his image in her hands, the fascination and resentment of an artist for her material and a jealous awe of his life-force, his power as a fountain of lifegiving news. She was famous for her interviews which were conducted whilst her subject was making love to her and consequently wide open emotionally, but Euri had so far managed to evade this ordeal. Since his marriage she had become very friendly with Chrys, who puzzled Euri by her tolerance. In deference to the formality of the occasion Leni was wearing the minimum of clothing: even so, her ample figure gave plenty of concealment for her recorder and TV.

Bubo joined them. He had cadged the last morsels of criticism and was sweating luxuriously. He greeted Chrys beaming and moist-eyed.

"A perfect round!" he said. "Not one missed! I spoke to everyone and knew all their names, all their children's names, their hobbies, their artistic gifts—and all from memory! Look. No recorders, no memovoice in my ear. And I knew everything that's happened to them in the course of the year. They appreciate that you know, Euri, though you prefer to be independent. They are glad to know that they do not suffer alone, that there is someone who cares. I remind them of things they've forgotten:

miseries cured, disasters averted, wrong turnings pointed out. I explain to them actions which seemed undemocratic at the time but which were directed to *someone's* good. They are glad to know that nothing, however small, escapes my consideration."

"You know us better than we know ourselves," Euri said unhappily. He saw Bubo in Eternity remembering and re-creating them for his own pleasure and their having to refer to him to find out who they were. From Congress Plaza he thought he heard a million-voiced groan but that could only be imagination. The winds would blow any sound away long before it could reach this height. Followed by the others he walked to the wall again and looked down at the Plaza. The light shone brighter as each newcomer brought his personal illumination. If all these people were joined by those not yet off shift and those now at Parties, Midnight would see a colossal disaster. He wondered why they were all huddling together when Liberation was coming to free them.

The others had turned their eyes to the night sky. Bubo bowed to Chrys: "How I look forward to seeing in the skies of Eternity the new constellations you will create!"

"I look forward to Eternity as a release from Art. Creation is not artistic. I shall let my world create itself."

She glanced at Euri and smiled but he could see she was not happy. A few scudding clouds that had escaped the Meteorological Army passed beneath them glowing palely in the moonlight.

"And what do you expect?" Leni asked, taking hold of Euri's arm.

"In a world where anything can happen we're freed from the tyranny of prediction."

"Yes, but what do you *expect*?"

The last thing he wanted was to explain his dreams to Leni. He pretended to take a red energy pill and scowled at her. She took the bait, shook out *two* red pills and swallowed them, expecting him to double up again and a first-rate hostile interview to take place. He smiled tranquilly and she saw she'd been bluffed. "What will Eternity be *like*?" she insisted in a rage.

Bubo broke in: "We have broken through the death-barrier. We can guarantee what earlier generations could only hope for—Paradise, individualized to your taste."

"Never to die," said Leni, who had had the presence of mind to tranquillize herself down to their level again. "How strange that seems. The medicos say they cannot guarantee the functioning of my body beyond the 29th May 2144. In Eternity I shall no longer shudder when May 29th comes round. There will *be* no May 29th's in my world!"

"And no 7th after Father's Day 2125!" Bubo cried.

"No 14th Christmas Shopping 2150!" said Chrys.

And no 10th of Summer 2145, thought Euri. Unlimited time! What problems could not be solved—disasters not forgotten? He took the green, sparkling glass Bubo offered and with the others drank to Eternity.

"And *all* our dreams will come true?" Leni persisted, looking at Euri. "We'll live in a world where all our desires are catered to, where we never grow old or stale, where there's always something new? New lovers, new desires?"

"Whatever you want you'll get," Euri said.

"And if I wanted *you*?"

"Chronophage can make you a simulacrum."

"But that won't be *you*!"

"It'll be what you want."

"I wonder?"

"We shall be immortal!" Euri said impatiently, thrusting his glass at Bubo to refill. "And if you wish, Eternity can be one long never-ending orgasm. Chronophage will constantly renew our bodies and therefore our desires. We'll be eternally young. We'll be omnipotent except that any aggression on others will be impossible due to their own omnipotence. Nobody can steal from us because we can re-create what is gone—perhaps without even knowing that we were stolen from. But we'll have no need to steal or harm, having everything we can desire. How can evil exist in Eternity? There'll be no need to do anything—only to be what we truly are. We'll be part of Nature once more—every breath of wind will carry out thoughts and every thought will stir the winds. There'll be no physical laws, no gravity, no cause and effect, no loss of energy. Without needing even to think we'll create a Universe in our own image and see our own happiness in everything.

"We shall *be* the Universe—eternal, boundless, never-ending. There'll be no Past to chain or torment us or to reach past us into the Future to take its revenge when we least expect it. Nothing that we do will have consequences or regrets. There'll be no need for cleverness—how weary I am of thinking! What use will intelligence be? Supermen have no need of intelligence. The brain was only a freak development of evolution to compensate us for more serious deficiencies. In Eternity there'll be no laws—only imagination and purpose."

He stopped abruptly, annoyed at giving himself away. He felt he was leaving Bubo and Leni a scent by which to pursue him through Eternity. And Chrys, staring through the glass wall, had withdrawn into the recesses of her own mind. The Party was unnaturally quiet. Some had wandered up and were smiling at him as if he were no more than a sport of their dream.

"Oh college days!" Bubo said, laughing. "How you carry me back. I can remember myself at the age of thirty in my ninth year of college. How I worked! You can look it up in my record. It's all there—my idealism, my desire to help the world. We used to argue through the night, my fellow students and I, living on pills alone for a month at a time, never sleeping. Our discussions were just like this—you'll find tapes of them in my public record—but even in the egotism of youth I knew that I would need those I helped as much as they needed me."

Euri detested Bubo in his 'more insightful than thou' mood. "What need do you think anyone will have of you when we can get anything we want?"

"My services may be more in demand than ever. You don't realize how much manpower is involved in keeping you happy. One new happiness creates a hundred new miseries. As a Servant I have had to become an *expert* in misery. We believe that Liberation will end this situation but if it holds true for Eternity then I dread what is to come."

"But shall we be able to help one another if we all live in our separate worlds?" Chrys asked, looking from Euri to Bubo impatiently.

"The theory is that when we are all united in Chronophage like will gravitate towards like," Bubo replied. "For instance, husbands and wives will share the same world—if they are well-matched. Chronophage will detect our thoughtwaves—strictly speaking our thoughtwaves and those of Chronophage will be distortions of the Earth's electromagnetic-gravitational field—and in accordance with those thoughtwaves reform into new patterns the atoms swarming round us, even in our own bodies. It's exactly the same principle that you'll have seen a hundred times on TV except that where the experimenter could only create objects in a small tank, due to the tremendous energies required, we shall have the whole world to experiment in."

"But the results weren't always satisfactory," Chrys said. "The experimenter didn't always get exactly what he wanted."

"We don't always know exactly what we want. That's where the knowledge that Chronophage has, the *entire* knowledge of the human race, comes in to substantiate your dream."

"Over the entire world?"

"Yes. Remember that even when we spread out over the surface of the globe we shall still occupy only a very thin skin and Chronophage will have all the energies in the iron ocean that stretches beneath the world to utilize. In any case, its powers are never likely to be strained to the limit since no two people are going to want the same thing at the same time. There'll be a constant flux of desire and negation. Where desires and ideas do coincide in broad essentials they will merge like streams flowing into one wide river. There'll be no concealment in Eternity. No one will be able to disguise himself. The unhappy will not be able to hide themselves from us and refuse our help."

Euri shut his ears to this explanation, praying that Bubo was wrong. His longing for Eternity oppressed him. His heart felt like a dam behind which flood waters were building up. He longed for release from all earthbound, heavy, short, weary, imprisoned things.

A gong sounded gently through the room and the heaving floor mushroomed into tables covered with a profusion of elaborate dishes and ornaments. The galleries of Magellan had been stripped to provide polished wood and real leather flasks for the wine.

"Just a foretaste of what we shall enjoy in Eternity," Bubo said. "Don't worry. The Brain has full details of these treasures and will be able to make a million perfect replicas."

Euri cared nothing for this kind of magnificence. He would have liked to sit and think of the radiant world of his imagining in peace but this was, to his disgust, always the moment chosen for speech-making. Those who were to speak put on their ceremonial spectacles that magnified the eyes to a soulful sincerity. (Across the back of the lenses, visible only to the wearer, ran the words of his speech.) Euri refused to make a speech and he had no cause to regret this for the robot authors had responded to the historic occasion with little new—machines had even less idea than men what Eternity would be like—and none of the speakers was able to shine. He listened to Bubo's speech with special attention in case there might be some official announcement, but Bubo had only his usual annual confession of misdeeds to make. This time he begged forgiveness for the whole course of his life and the entire audience, moved to tears, recorded an immediate vote of confidence and showered him with yellow happiness pills. He swallowed a handful in respectful acknowledgement and, swelling with pleasure, sat down again at the table he shared with Chrys, Euri and his wife.

"Everything is going wonderfully well," he said. "I attach greater importance to this last Party than perhaps you realize. Last year's was not successful—you remember the chicken?"

Leni laughed: "The synthesized chicken?"

"That's what was alleged. In fact I am convinced it was real chicken. All my enquiries have led me to believe that. The matter was a very serious one indeed. If we *had* been deluded it meant that some terrible, some unbelievable psychological disaster had overtaken the College of Culinarians. Not only that but the way our tolerance of the rumour showed a basic distrust in the Universal Society alarmed me. A thorough investigation was held under a Congressional Licence."

"The chicken was nothing like as good as we'd been led to believe real chicken would be, though," Euri said.

"But few of the luxuries of the primitive world have ever lived up to expectations. Those oranges we had the year before turned out to be poor dry things and the rice that we've read so much about was tasteless. Give me supersaturated hydroponic fruit-tissue any time. However, the credibility of our society is at stake. Distrust and disillusion spread like radio-active weed."

"Can't you forget all this now that the world's coming to an end?"

"Lack of faith in society is lack of faith in oneself. Believe me, I went into all the rumours with feelings of despair. They said we had been duped with plastic meat, porcelain bones, a rubber skin. I began to hear again that real chicken was of an indescribable deliciousness. Consequently I have arranged a demonstration which will convince all of you that this year you are eating real chicken."

Bubo rose to his feet in a dead silence and, lit by an invisible spotlight which made him brilliant, walked over to the wall and pushed a button. A long glass-enclosed tank in the wall which had not been observable before was illuminated. It began where Bubo stood and almost completed a circuit of the room before ending in a red glow over a table covered with plates not far from Bubo.

Now they heard a strange gabbling like an alienated TV. Smiling, Bubo donned gauntlets, reached gingerly down into a large box and then, quickly standing up, held out at arm's length something that rattled in his hands. No one in the room had ever seen a live chicken except on TV when it had first been announced that this life-form had been reconstructed from dried egg powder discovered in an ancient war-cache. There was a shout of laughter.

After a few moments Bubo, with every appearance of relief, hastily dropped the creature into the tank which, they could now see, was a kind of runway. Impelled by electric shocks, the chicken made a circuit of the room so that everyone could get a fair look at it. Its really ludicrous squawkings were amplified and filled the room with increasing amusement. Something about the bird's erratic and grotesquely emotional cries touched a common nerve. The diners laughed until the tears came and some screamed. Bubo waved the bird round the runway as if he had composed its comic progress. In the brightly-lit tank the bird scampered furiously to its doom, oblivious of the diners who shouted *'Look out!'* and laughed louder as the bird, maddened by the shocks, ran faster.

Leni approached the runway to take close-up shots and soon Euri and Chrys, who remained silent at their table, could see on their TV the bird in close-up, its actions artistically speeded to a hilarious explosion of feathers and immediately afterwards the same sequence slowed to a dreamlike balletic floating. It was beautiful TV: impartial, rounded, showing the subject from a thousand viewpoints, scrupulously fair to all the possibilities inherent in the chicken's actions. Meanwhile the chicken was approaching the end of the runway.

The wild applause was silenced at the sight of a pair of loosely dangling steel claws waiting at the end of the runway. At the bird's approach they galvanized into action. They seized it and silenced it. Euri sighed with relief when the noisy bird, reduced to a lump of meat revolving in an infra-red glow, moved towards the serving hatch where it popped out on to a plate. Chrys had not uttered a sound. Bubo carried the roast chicken to the furthest table.

Bubo despatched chicken after chicken to the diners whose hilarity increased rather than diminished as the spectacle grew familiar. Euri and Chrys refused the roast chicken Bubo brought them.

"They don't feel anything," he assured Chrys anxiously. "Their reactions are purely automatic."

"A little *too* automatic?" Euri suggested angrily.

"You're expecting a lot of a chicken!"

"It could be another fake—a film sequence. The predictability of all their actions! Not one of those birds has acted in the least differently—and that meaningless noise!"

"Do you think I'm fooling you? Come and see for yourself. You can do it yourself."

"No thanks."

"What else can the chicken do?" Bubo asked. "It cannot endure the electric shocks and its only escape from them is along the runway. It cannot break out of the runway. It cannot escape the claws or the oven. One imagines that it could accept its fate with more dignity but that is no concern of ours. We only care what it tastes like."

"It seems to me to taste much like last year's chicken," Leni said, without enthusiasm.

"Well that is what I set out to prove, after all," Bubo said gloomily. "What a thankless occupation mine is! To relieve disappointment I have to confirm that disappointment existed! If I prove that you were not disappointed in the *reality* of the chicken I have to disappoint you in your *expectation* of reality. Don't you understand why I fear Eternity? What infinite disappointment! What unlimited despair you may know!"

The rest of the birds were thrown together into the runway. They scrambled towards their death, impeding each other in their desire to be first. The sight maddened Euri. He snatched a heavy dish from the table and hurled it with all his strength at the glass runway. He was shaking with rage and fear. The glass shattered extensively.

The loudspeakers fell silent and through the silence the chickens' unamplified cries sounded feebly, soon to be accompanied by a similar noise which the bewildered diners did not at first associate with the flame-petals fluttering from the oven. A second later the bright lights were replaced by the dull glow of emergency non-electric lighting and the flames sprang into prominence and crackled loudlier. An alarm startled them all from their hypnotized stupor. The tables hastily retreated into the floor, leaving people sprawling. Emergency exits threw themselves open but few took advantage of them. Half the diners took out their TV cameras and began to record the scene like one-eyed devouring giants: the others willingly performed for them, copying Euri and sending plates smashing into the glass. The noise was stupendous: cheers, screams, breaking glass, the purposeful roar of the fire, the subdued mutter of the chickens.

Leni was by now relayed direct to the Press Academy computer. She seized Euri and asked in the accusing tone of her profession: "Will you tell us why you smashed the glass, Euri Sir?"

"It was a symbolic act . . ." Euri began but there came an almost inaudible buzz and Leni checked him.

"O.K. We can take it from there. The Press Academy computer will expand and complete your statement in accordance with your registered views and positions."

She rushed round the room and within a minute had conducted a dozen similar interviews.

By now the destruction that Euri had begun was completed. People had turned to throwing things at the robots who were rushing to the source of the fire which was now spreading round the room and blackening the glass dome above. Down the walls and across the floor dribbled a heavy yellow anti-fire smoke which soon came up to their ankles. Through this smoke scurried the chickens Euri had freed, making desperate leaps, running in circles, some throwing themselves back into the higher-leaping flames, skidding, screeching, sending the yellow smoke swirling and eddying, acting in as mad, random, incoherent and individual a way as even Euri could approve.

Under attack from the chickens most of the diners panicked and rushing out the emergency exits jumped into the panic-sacks in which they would be delivered, sleepily drugged, to their own apartments. Euri himself felt a surge of irrational fear. The animals that roamed Magellan were not like these: neurosectomy made them mild and pacific. But these creatures ran straight at people, stabbed at their legs and snarled at them. It was a terrifying experience.

"Why are they behaving like this?" Leni shouted angrily.

Bubo, looking with undisguised anger at Euri, replied: "Their brains were not treated. There seemed no need to do so since they were destined for food and not for pets and also there would have been nothing convincing or entertaining about them if they had been treated."

Euri jumped up and waving his arms chased the chickens towards the exits that were still open, waiting for the few remaining diners to escape. He had no success. He found himself only running round in circles and driving the birds crazier. The level of the smoke was rising and now almost covered the chickens that swam through it.

"What do you think you're doing?" Bubo shouted. "Haven't you done enough already?"

The Party had certainly been ruined.

"Look! They're dying," Chrys said, pointing to where a madly-struggling bird had sent a cloud of smoke spiralling in intricate writhing convolutions. "*There's* Art for you—what vigour! What poetry! What communication!"

Euri took her arm. She was trembling uncontrollably. Leni turned away and either from tact or some other emotion forbore to record her emotion. Euri gripped her arm tightly and she cried out in pain: "I can't stand any more of this. Let's get out of here."

However she willingly took a tranquillizer that Bubo offered and he took the opportunity to say: "Won't you come with us to welcome the New Era? Come, Euri, you owe us that."

"We can't let you go," Leni said. "Chrys is in no shape to face Liberation alone. You'd better stay here: all the mobile hospitals will be stationed round here at Midnight."

"If there's anyone to man them," Euri said.

"Some of us will retain a sense of duty even though our society expires," Bubo retorted.

Slowly the commotion of the chickens was subsiding; allegro, adagio, they drowned in the yellow smoke.

Euri looked round. There were only the four of them left in the domed room, surrounded by protective robots.

Liberation!

The fire extinguished, the fire-robots returned to their posts under the floor. The TV informed them that an audience of 17 million had watched their ordeal. Now that the fire was out the room was in semi-darkness. They walked out on to the roof where the fliers were parked. The moon shone down on them, small and bright like a balloon that had floated clear above the city. They looked up at it as at an old memory. And at that moment it was blotted out by the simultaneous explosion of ten thousand fireworks celebrating Liberation. The light swamped the city and turned it momentarily into a tropical coral formation and the fliers into darting fish.

"In a few hours," Euri whispered to Chrys, "all this will be the least meaningful thing in our experience. We shall forget life here just as we forget a bad dream."

"And will *we* be no more than creatures from your nightmare?" Leni asked spitefully.

"Euri mistakes, as always, a momentary wish for a fundamental longing," Bubo said soothingly. "His social health is much better than he likes us to believe. He will not forget us. We are essential furniture of his mind. I'm sure he'll welcome us into his Eternity."

"What do you know of my thoughts and desires?" Euri addressed Bubo with a bitter but increasingly triumphant contempt. "You know *nothing* of what a 100%DCS is capable of. Haven't your spies told you how long I've been free of you?"

He laughed when he saw Bubo's bewilderment. He felt free, in command. He had nothing to fear now that Liberation was only a few watches away. He felt almost giddy with the intense relief that filled him. He had thrown off his secret and with it allegiance to Magellan and all it stood for. Bubo was silent.

The building seemed to shudder in the blast from the fireworks. The squally glare of the primitive chemical light sent a hundred expressions tumbling over the faces of the others. Euri was drunk with the sensation of his freedom: like a drunkard he was determined that Bubo should appreciate and participate in his joy.

"Liberation is almost here," he said, "and you too, my Servant, will have to face Eternity. Alone. Without me. Shall I show you how far I've gone beyond all cure? As a gesture of goodwill?"

Bubo looked back towards the dome where, by all tradition, the diners ought now to have been copulating on the tables. He sighed.

"We have several watches left before Midnight and you've destroyed the Party. Yes, show us what you mean."

The 'us' made Euri pause in momentary uncertainty. He had forgotten that his revelations would come as an equally unexpected shock to Chrys. However, the sudden sobering of his intoxication was so chilling that he knew he would have to continue. Besides, he could not have entered

Eternity without telling Chrys.

"Do you want to know?" he asked her.

She nodded. Leni had camera in hand already so without further hesitation Euri called a flier over to them and gave it the instructions: 17,41,62.

"The Old City!" Leni protested, outraged.

The flier awaited a consensus.

"Well all right then, but we must be back here at Midnight. I've no desire to meet Eternity in the Old City!"

Before proceeding they halted the flier over Congress Plaza at a lower level. Seeing that huge area crammed with so many people they were silent with amazement at first. Visibility was restricted by the haze and the explosions of the fireworks and the light that came from all directions and blinded them, but from moment to moment fresh vistas opened up and showed the crowd stretching as far as they could see. Now they understood what was meant by the phrase 'population pressure' they had heard so much of this last year.

"I see why we had to break through into Eternity," Chrys said wonderingly.

"Yet we've had birth stabilization for decades," Leni said. "This problem must have been with us for a long time. Why didn't we just create another Magellan—somewhere in the ocean, say?"

"And divide the human race again?" Bubo said. "What few divisions we have already—for instance, the Academies—cause friction and rivalry. Set up another City! First you'd have a proposal for artistic competition, then local welfare offices, next a bigger share of whatever we had, finally, autonomy and War! No, better Eternity with all its risks."

The canals still flowed and they could see the slow circling of the crowd and the turbulence caused by struggles for vantage points. Most faces were turned upwards as if Liberation was expected to come from the sky. Euri felt a unique sensation of awe and fear at the mystery of the crowd's latent desires. He was surprised to hear Leni describing the same emotions fluently into her microphone.

"Liberation is here already," Bubo said. "The world can never be the same again. The promise is as powerful as the fact."

They stooped lower. At this height the flier was battered by the splintering stars and rocked in the wakes of rockets that screamed upwards *Liberation! Liberation!* to the sky and, exploding in deafening claps of laughter, rained incense on the city. The crowd was in more violent motion than they had realized and now they could see the bodies of deer and tigers that had been unable to escape to the deserted outlying streets, crushed and trampled.

"They're going crazy down there!" Leni gasped and hurriedly she got in touch with the Press Academy but there was no report of what they could see. "That's strange. . . . Of course we're seeing only a small part of the broad overall picture. This cannot be representative."

"Would you prefer to stay and record this historic scene?" Euri asked.

"It can't be important. Let's get to wherever we're going."

The city shimmered and fractured like a reflection in choppy water. The air was electric. The flier was tossed in air-eddies, jolted by rocket-explosions, its brain confused by lightening flashes and radio incoherence. It moved away with alacrity towards the outskirts of the city.

The outlying parts already looked dead and the frontier

of the Old City was no longer so strongly marked. Even Euri, who had always thought he hated Magellan, was affected by the sight of its death—for it *was* death. It looked irreversible. The Past was crumbling and still they had no clear view of the Future. Between the Now and Midnight Euri felt an increasing claustrophobia as of walls closing in. The flier swooped rapidly over the barrier of warehouses and beautification zones and then spiralled down to halt for a second in an ancient surface station. The others, whose first experience of the Old City this was, looked out with apprehensive interest at signboards indicating destinations they'd never heard of.

Plastic and glass lay scattered in thick dust and fungus. At one end the station had either collapsed or been pulled down and they averted their eyes as they would have done if someone had collapsed in the street. Disappointingly there was nothing of value. Long ago, collectors had stripped the Old Posters from the walls. By now the flier was hurtling a few inches above rusting rails through a desolation that exemplified every meaning of the word 'obscene' as these citizens of Magellan understood it—dead, dark, diseased, shameless. Soon they came to a halt at another station just outside the main ruins of the Old City and the flier told them they had arrived at their goal. But nothing had lit up at their approach, no route was indicated. The others looked at Euri in helpless disgust.

Ordering the flier to wait he led the way out of the station. He had kept his light on him since the morning—perhaps he had intended all along to revisit the Casino?—and though the others didn't disguise their horror of the dark masses that surrounded them, and the unnerving way they changed position as he moved the light, he kept steadily on. He'd brought the flier as near as he could to the Casino. He had never approached it so openly above ground before and he was amazed to see several lines of footsteps in the thick dust. He followed them, holding his light high and saying nothing about this extraordinary discovery. The others trooped behind in silence, none anxious to lose him in the dark, dank, evil-smelling, crumbling street. He took none of his usual precautions. Midnight and the presence of a Servant and critico made secrecy pointless. What would the Gamblers think? He laughed and laughed again as he turned and saw the others, bewildered and dismayed.

He was looking for an entrance to the underground river that he knew ought to be somewhere near here. He followed the footsteps until they vanished in an open windswept space. Continuing in the same direction he soon recognized a maintenance-station of the old pattern. Inside its entrance the footsteps recommenced. He glanced at Chrys. She was looking pale but determined. He was not happy at having to take her underground but it was the route he knew best and he hadn't time to waste stumbling over the concrete-rubble mountains of the surface. Also, and not less important, he wanted to exorcize his lingering fear of the underground and he believed her presence would help him. Ignoring their protests he led the way into the narrow corridor and showed them the hatch and iron ladder. A body-rotting ice-wind blew up the shaft but they had to follow Euri or be left behind in the street, lost amidst those featureless, tumbled ruins.

The underground river brought gasps of astonishment from Chrys and Leni. Down in the tunnel the last sounds of Magellan were silenced. They moved without speaking, terrified by the ghosts that had accompanied them all their lives and never revealed themselves until now. They stared with blank eyes at the flat black water below, the curved grey ceiling, the rusty wasting inspectionway leading into darkness.

The Euri who had come this way twelve hours ago was another man. The present Euri was anxious to see for himself what had been experienced by that other man. He had only a stranger's confused explanations of what had happened. He hurried on and back.

"You know the way well," Chrys said sadly.

"Why in sanity's name do we have to go this way?" Leni, close behind, asked.

"The Old City was pretty well atomized in the War. There are mountains of rubble which can only be crossed with climbing equipment. Fliers can't get low enough or land."

Bubo added to this explanation with an excessively loud confidence: "There are a few rough roads for maintenance patrols and archaeological expeditions but for obvious psychological reasons we don't encourage interest in the immediate pre-war period."

At last Euri came to a familiar turning and paused to take breath. The others looked at him from shadowed eyes.

"And you've been here many times?" Leni said.

"Yes."

"That's strange. There's no sign of life here. I'd never have guessed that anyone had passed through here since the time of the ancients."

She gazed intensely at Euri as if she doubted his being animate. He took a few paces into the narrow passageway and then put out his light. In front of him a faint glow suggested itself. Leni pushed past him and ran towards it. She shouted to them excitedly to come as she found the fracture in the wall—the original entrance, reinforced and barred, still stood firm beside it—and scrambled through it. They followed eagerly. Outside, half the sky was filled with the celebration fires of Magellan. All thoughts of the tunnel were stilled as they stared in awe.

"The War must have looked like that," Chrys said. She sighed deeply as if she hadn't drawn breath since leaving Magellan.

Soon, however, the silence and darkness behind them drew them away from that violent spectacle. They found they were now in the heart of the Old City, the moon outlining the ruins in an ancient flat monochrome. Leni cried out in fear. Buildings swayed over them with the terrifying threat of millions of tons of unsupported steel and masonry in insecure balance. Some steelframed buildings, warped out of true, spilled out their floors like a chest-of-drawers. These buildings sang, not with the vibrations of channelled energy, but wearily and randomly as the winds chose to attack them. Everywhere drifted a rank smell from the rotting vegetation that grew in every crack and crevice, every weak point, like a disease. There was a chill here that in all their lives they'd never known, a cancer that ate away the body of the Old City and so contaminated it that once touched by the disease it could never be restored to truth.

Leni was openly afraid: "Why wasn't all this destroyed and sterilized? What are we being exposed to?"

"The danger is infinitesimal," Euri said. "There's probably less radiation here than we get in Magellan from our atomic engines and electronic devices. Most of what seems alien and diseased to you is simply weeds and wildflowers that were common before the War. This is the only place left for them to grow. In any case, the use of a nuclear sterilization burst so close to Magellan would be unthinkable. And besides, Magellan shares a number of lifelines with the Old City—like the river you've just seen which acts as a sewer for us. It would have taken another twenty years to build Magellan if the founding fathers had had to begin from scratch."

"But the health risk, the psychological risk!" Leni said, turning accusingly to Bubo.

"We knew this," Bubo said. He was shivering slightly and as he caught Euri's eye he looked angry and then menacing. He was standing on a beam of concrete, off-balance and uncertain. "Yes, I was always aware that there were dangers in such an unnatural environment but I must admit I never *felt* it as we're experiencing it now. If I had had any idea of its virulence I would have insisted on the whole area being sealed off. The fact is—I may as well tell you now that Liberation will end its value—we considered the Old City to be a valuable and unique study-area. Things go on in here that would never come to the surface and show themselves in the light of Magellan. Nowhere else could we determine so easily the symptoms of the various diseases that afflict modern man.

"Yes, Euri," he continued with confident compassion, "your Gamblers have been known to us for a considerable time, long before you knew them, in fact. It was I who directed your footsteps to the Casino: you would never have heard of it if it had not been for me. I hoped to bring your disease to a crisis so that I could cure it, but your illness is deep-rooted and Liberation has come quicker than anyone expected. . . . Even so, now that I *see* and *feel* the Old City for myself . . . I wonder if I was right?"

Euri had long trained himself never to react to any statement or innuendo of Bubo's but this stunningly direct revelation caught him unprepared. He stood motionless, one arm half-raised, as introspective as a dummy in a shop window. His first thought had been a very conventional outrage that his Servant could have knowingly allowed him to undergo such an emotio-moral dislocation but then, overwhelming all other feelings, like a flash flood tearing away feeble growths that have established themselves in a dry channel, came a rage that left him weak from its violence. *He had never been free!* He stepped towards Bubo hardly knowing what he intended to do but checked himself as Bubo shrank back. He looked guiltily at the others but his and Bubo's actions must have been less dramatic than he'd imagined for they appeared to have noticed nothing and to be listening to Bubo in bewilderment. Bubo knew about the Gamblers!

He heard Leni say something in a tone of angry disappointment, then he turned his back on them and continued frantically to lead the way along a well-marked path through the rubble that eventually wound behind a large square building.

"The Space Museum?" Bubo, trotting behind him, asked.

"You know it!"

Euri was distracted from his turmoiling emotions by the prickling of the skin that meant they were under electronic surveillance. He had had no time to decide how to act, so all he could do was to behave as if the situation was unchanged. His first desire to turn back to Magellan had been replaced by a determination to find out just how true Bubo's words had been. He halted.

"We wait here. The entrance is never in the same place twice. It's a kind of maze the doorkeeper can modify a hundred ways. One never learns the way in or out."

As he spoke a green light shone round them and even Euri, who'd been expecting it, shuddered. They turned to see a crazily-tilted entrance into which, following Euri, they descended. They walked along two or three turnings and then into a small room which spun round and sank. After a short descent a door opened on to a featureless ante-room which contained a single masked attendant armed with a quiver of poisoned metal-fibre burrs. Euri had expected trouble in accounting for the others but not even the password was demanded and he was glad that a precaution which would have been so humiliating after Bubo's disclosures had been dispensed with. The attendant approached them with a tray in his hand.

"Now you have to give up any pills, capsules, anything you're carrying to ensure a selected emotion," Euri said.

"But why?" Leni asked, for once embarrassed at such an indecent request. She had stepped forward wearing her palm-print detector gloves to shake hands with the attendant but he'd ignored her, and even if he had shaken hands with her no voice from the Press Academy would have whispered in her ear that the attendant was Citizen So-and-so, for the Casino was insulated against radio waves. Euri began to feel in command once more.

"You are now in the Casino—a different world from yours. We insist on complete mental nakedness. Without that you can't respond to different orders of experience. You can't *feel* anything new or real when you take drugs to make them conform to what you have decided upon beforehand."

"But I'm a critico. I have to remain apart from the actions I describe."

"You won't be reporting this."

"But why trouble to go through with this ridiculous charade now that Bubo has told us it's merely another therapy-session? Besides, we've all taken hundreds of different pills in the course of the day: nobody *ever* faces life naked! We could far better go without food or warmth."

"If you want to enter you must do as I say. This is a serious matter. The drugs you've already taken will soon wear off. If you can't conform to our rules then you'll have to wait here or return to Magellan on your own."

After varying mental struggles they each complied. They followed Euri to a door which disclosed itself now—Leni holding her hand to her head as if already she felt the first twinges of an anxiety-storm.

"All this reminds me of the socially-incoherent I spent my intern period with," Bubo muttered, "but worse—much worse. *Their* struggles were to achieve happiness, balance, integration. But this is utterly perverse, anti-social, reactionary—a deliberate, self-induced disease. This *secrecy*, these codes and mystifications, these opaque, claustrophobic enclosures!—what do they mean?"

Euri did not reply. Hearing the overtones of disquiet in Bubo's voice, he experienced an almost innocent elation. And Bubo had not yet seen the half of it! He threw the door wide open and watched Bubo and Leni as they struggled against the shame and nausea that the Space Museum induced in them. He avoided looking at Chrys.

They had entered the main exhibition structure of the

Space Museum, an enormous hall filled with rockets similar to those that had devastated the world. Everything that was evil was towering above them, hundreds of feet high, grotesque, alien, sardonic presences, the Moonrockets, Solar Observatories, transPlutonian reconnaissance ships. The heat of their bodies evaporated into the vast coldness and their blood turned to ice: they shivered in atavistic fear of the cold outer worlds and an Earth consumed in fire. The ships pointed into the darkness into which the parabolic vaulting soared with an inhuman, monomaniac purposefulness.

"Madness! Madness!" Bubo whispered.

"Primitive words!" Euri jeered.

"Primitive words for primitive facts."

"They can't harm you. Look closely. You see? They're dead. That stuff that looks like dried blood on their sides is only rust. Their lives were finished when they were brought here, and even when they were working their designs were nothing that you could understand."

They looked again and saw that the barbaric machines were truly indifferent to them. Euri wondered if Chrys also felt that sense of complex loss which was so familiar to him, but he didn't dare ask for fear that she would look at him blankly and strangely.

As their eyes grew accustomed to the scale of the spaceships they saw, unnoticed against their bulk, spidery ladders and lifts that ran up the sides towards tiny trapdoors; entrances to a thousand hells.

"Which would you like to enter?" Euri asked maliciously.

"None!"

"They say that people who enter never return but that's

not true."

"Have *you* explored them?"

"I entered one," Euri admitted unhappily.

"No wonder you're ill."

"It was strange but not so terrible, after all. Difficult to realize it had been intended for men, though. No room to move or stand upright. Dials and controls on the ceiling and floor—anywhere but where you'd expect them. Very uncouth in layout and far from sophisticated—more like a very old-fashioned flier than anything. I'm sure we could build infinitely better machines. Poor materials. No taste or imagination. No convenience—not a sign of any provision for entertainment. Empty. Bare. Possibly the furnishings were removed before it came here. Everything was covered in some white growth and the thin plating almost eaten through. It was when I discovered that that I came out in a hurry: I was frightened of falling through the floor and being trapped in the trunk of the rocket. No one would have dared come to find me. Perhaps that's what happened to others."

"Did you find freedom or happiness there?" Bubo asked.

"No, but . . ."

"The ancients were swallowed by these cannibal machines," Leni said, authoritatively. "Thank God we have Chronophage to protect us from ours!"

"They too were trying to discover Eternity," Euri said. Looking up at those great but fragile cocoons he felt Time waiting to snatch him with steel claws. *Liberation!*

"But is this *all* you brought us to see?" Leni asked with outraged contempt. "Is this what you were boasting about?"

"Not altogether. Look there!"

The others turned without reluctance from the spaceships and looked into the distant confusion of irrational shapes and colours that were scattered over the vast floor until they spotted movement and saw with astonishment that all this time a quite sizable but silent crowd, insignificant under the spaceships, had occupied part of the hall. There were several hundred people there, far more than were usually present, and Euri understood now who had left the footprints he'd seen on the way.

"What's that in the middle? It looks like a Cube for a Ball Game," Leni asked.

"That's what it is."

"And you've brought us here to watch amateur Art?"

"This is different. Come on!" Euri said. "This isn't Art. We've tried to return to a truly primitive ideal of Sport. You know the simple principles of ancient athletic competition? Of course they long ago became merely contests between rival drug manufacturers—I myself once ran the mile in two minutes—and then our economy ended even that and athletics became aesthetics. However we claim no aesthetic achievement. The sole interest of the Game for us lies in the intervention of a Third Party—*Fate*. We reject the reconciliation of Art."

While the others were puzzling over this explanation he led them over to the crowd which seemed to the others much like any audience at a festival, heads nodding, agreeing with each other that the nominal loser had yet been the greater player-stylist. But Euri saw with a sense of sacrilege that they were nearly all strangers. It hadn't occurred to him that other Gamblers would bring their friends to this last performance. They seemed to him to be soft and contemptuously amused in their ignorance.

"I don't understand," Leni persisted. "If there's no Art what's the point of it all? Don't tell us you've returned to playing to win or lose—what possible meaning can all that have in this modern age?"

"A very conclusive meaning for the loser. He's crippled or dies."

They looked at him, unsure of his meaning.

He repeated: "I mean *dies* literally—PRC's."

"Permanent Relinquishment of Citizenship!"

"Nonsense!" Leni said. "There's no injury the Game can inflict that would lead anywhere near such an extremity, and even if it could there's no injury that can't be repaired. We haven't had an accidental Loss of a citizen in two decades. At this moment there's ten thousand brains alone in cold storage. Why, it's been proved a hundred times that a citizen in good standing, with his records kept up to date, simply can't be permanently removed: even if your records are not in order and your new brain can only be brought up to last year there are always your friends to tell you what you are."

"But as I'm trying to tell you—we don't choose to repair. All we have here are simple medical facilities to enable the crippled to get to where they can fake an accident to account for their condition. But if death comes we accept it. We accept our Fate. We play the Game with different equipment—you'll see—and we play under different rules. The only prize for which we're playing is PRC—we prefer the old-fashioned word Death."

"This isn't Fate," Bubo protested, "but Voluntary Relinquishment!"

"We have that right under the Constitution."

"You also have the right to trained advice, motive-analysis at the deepest level, a probationary waiting period and, if all else fails, a non-traumatic PRC."

"We reject all these benefits."

Bubo and Leni laughed in exasperation. Chrys looked alert and grave. Somehow her unsmiling acceptance of what he said seemed a more damaging criticism than the jibes of the others.

"Have you any idea how ignorant you are?" Bubo asked, completely forgetting the normal courtesy demanded of a Servant, his voice thin and unresonant in the enormous vaulted hall. "Have you *died*? *I* have! Every Servant undergoes the experience of death at least once in the course of his training. The experience is considered of the utmost importance in formulating ideals."

"I'm glad you agree with us."

"The experience of one's *own* death, not that of others! How can dead men be of importance to us? The experience is only of value to those who survive it—and can only be administered to stable personalities, I may say. If you had only *asked* me I could have saved you all this! Death is *nothing*—complete cessation—not even loss. When I was revivified I knew that I was nothing except in relation to my fellow men. If it hadn't been for others keeping time I wouldn't have even known that I'd been dead. I lay down on the couch and was awakened immediately, as it seemed to me, but the world around me had moved on an entire year! When you've had that experience you cling to your fellow men, respect their opinions, seek their love and recognition! We are nothing without them! Even when you say you accept your Fate you're wrong. It's your fellow-Gamblers who accept death for you and who, in the ultimate analysis, must be rejecting and even *disliking* you."

"No!" Euri shouted. "It's we who reject the Universal Society. We're revolutionaries!"

"But we're all revolutionaries! Our society is in a permanent state of revolution. We're constantly seeking criticism. We look for dissatisfaction—we need its stimulus. Tell us your needs and join us in the revolution against that very Fate you worship! Don't you understand that it's *you* who are the reactionary? *We* are the true revolutionaries."

"Yes," Euri said. "That's why we had to keep *our* revolution secret. But for Liberation I should never have revealed the conspiracy."

Bubo looked at him compassionately. Some of the crowd had turned to listen to their argument. He lowered his voice and spoke so that only the other three could hear.

"But your actions have never been a secret to me. How did you imagine you could go unnoticed? We need you and we miss you when you are gone. No, we Servants are not 'dictators' or 'bureaucrats' or any other kind of ancient tyrant with selfish desires and interests to promote. Our interest is solely in *you*. We're guaranteed one hundred per cent altruistic observers, undistracted by purposes of our own. Consequently, you reveal yourself to us in every blind, egotistic action. We knew about this place from its very beginning, from its very *conception*, for we detected, long before it could make its appearance in less sensitive egoes, the psychosocial malaise and predicted the Game. You are not unique. There have been many like you."

"You knew this was going on," Leni said curiously, "and you did nothing about it?"

"There's no such thing as a perfectly healthy society,"

Bubo replied. "Where there's life there's disease and it's far better to allow diseases to come to their crisis-point away from Magellan. If this particular one had been repressed it would have shown up in a thousand places in Magellan itself—like acne in an adolescent. Usually we step in before these underground movements reach the point of ritual sacrifice and steer them back into amateur sports clubs, after which they invariably die a natural death.

"Despite what Euri says, this particular group had not yet reached that danger point, in my judgement. Since Euri was involved the affair was—and still is—under my personal supervision. I receive daily reports from Infiltrators. Our best assessment of the crisis-date was some three days hence, when the whole problem would be solved by the advent of Eternity. Unfortunately, I hadn't made sufficient allowance for the pressure, the *shock-wave*, of approaching Liberation.

"The first sacrifice came last night . . ."

"*Sacrifice?*" Leni echoed. "That disappearance last night was a *PRC*?"

"*You* knew also?" Euri cried in bewilderment.

"Relinquishments of citizen privileges can't be kept secret from the Press Academy."

"You *knew* there was a man killed here last night?" Euri repeated, gazing stupidly at Bubo, praying that these statements were simply tricks to obtain the psychological advantage.

"Of course."

Emotions so entangled he couldn't begin to recognize them individually swarmed at him. He reached for his tranquillizers and swore when he recalled they'd been taken. He grabbed hold of Bubo's arm and dragged him through the crowd to confront him with the brutal evidence of the Game. Chrys and Leni pushed their way anxiously after them. They reached the glass wall of the Cube but no Game was yet in progress. Euri stared idiotically in at the empty Cube.

Leni spoke to her husband in cold rage: "Why wasn't I informed? Do you think you're above the Freedom of the Press? Don't you know I could have you broken for status-aggravation and sent to a holiday-camp for the rest of your life? It's lucky for you that Liberation is nearly here! This would have been the biggest human drama in fifty years—and I had to miss it!"

"It was a matter of medical ethics," Bubo said, deeply embarrassed. "And since the subject was still under investigation and no treatment had been yet recommended, FP wasn't *technically* operative."

The crowd surged in their direction and they were pressed against the Cube. Euri was distracted and dismayed by the crazy excitement in the crowd's eyes, so different from the solemnity with which the Gamblers invoked Fate. Two men had just entered the Cube by an entrance that was sealed behind them.

When Euri saw the two Gamblers he knew—despite Bubo—that they were worth his allegiance. Their eyes burned with a steady fire, not the uncontrollable blaze one saw in the eyes of those whose life-force suddenly went nova and consumed itself desperately before medical aid could intervene—for cures were so rapid these days that illnesses had to be quicker still and a man might go mad and die in front of your eyes—no, the Gamblers were different: their purpose, their repose in the awful laws of Fate, gave them an *intelligence* that transcended any excellences they had as citizens of the Universal Society.

A blue light winked and the player in the blue mask picked up a small, shiny sphere from the centre of the floor.

"Blue has the ball," Euri said, calm now that the Game had started.

"Why?"

"No reason. A computer geared to a variable field of reference—probably the complex wave-pattern of the heart-beats of the audience—selects blue or red with 99·98 per cent unpredictability."

"Pure chance? No justice? No equality-distribution? What if the more skilful player gets first go?"

"We believe this to be a higher equality."

The basics of the Game were familiar to them all. The four walls and ceiling of the Cube were positively energized so that the ball rebounded from them at a uniform velocity no matter how hard it struck them. So long as the ball continued to hit one of these five sides it would remain in motion but as soon as it touched the negatively energized floor it would come to a dead halt. Players had alternate throws or fought for possession. A time-limit to the wall energization was also usual.

"I can't see any scoreboard," Leni said.

"Scoring is on one's opponent's body—the ball is solid silver."

Leni laughed incredulously and angrily. She hated to be made fun of. Now the two players began. The ball streaked round the Cube—as soon vanished from the eye's focus as a shooting star. Leni saw no sign of scoring and soon began to grow restless. She tried to push out of the crowd but could not budge it. She opened her mouth to make it listen to her but as she did so Blue Mask received the ball full in the chest and her voice was drowned in the crowd's scream.

Blue had been darting forward but when the ball hit him he stopped as if he'd run into a glass wall, coughed and crumpled to the floor like a deactivated robot. He lay still in a sudden dead silence, then a stream of blood poured over his lips and down the side of his face and the crowd shrieked with joy.

"Blood! Suffering! Must we wallow in *all* the obscenities?" Bubo shouted.

Euri had nothing to say. The man he had killed had been struck a glancing blow on the temple and had died as if quitting the insubstantial armour of his body. The usual injuries caused by the Game were broken limbs and internal injuries that did not result in blood. Blue's soul seemed to be drowning in the puddle of blood. The two women were staring dumbly at this disgusting sight.

"Bubo is right," he said at last. "There were no deaths before last night. We Gamblers aren't suicidal after all. No true Gambler will take risks greater than 50:50—we want an *equal* partnership with Fate. Those who take greater risks are abusing the Game. There's something very strange about this place tonight. No one will play another if his skill is very much superior. A player like Red should never have been in the Cube with Blue. . . . Wait a moment. . . ." He struggled through the crowd to the only fellow Gambler he recognized and when he returned told them blankly: "Something's gone wrong. There's been three deaths already tonight. This isn't what I meant you to see. Death isn't really the point. It's the *challenge*. . . ."

"You don't follow your own argument through," Bubo said, contemptuously. "Tonight you stand to lose not just a few years of inessential life but Eternity itself. This was never philosophy but only a disease you contracted. Look at these people here—don't you see that they'll know no peace until they've destroyed themselves? Make haste if you want to join them because I'm going to call a halt to this!"

"You can't stop us!"

"I have this place under protective surveillance."

"You can't have us that closely watched or else you couldn't have allowed these men to die and lie so long—they'll never be revived before Midnight. They've escaped you!"

Bubo was silent but to an indignant question from Leni he admitted: "Yes, it's true. I couldn't afford to alert the Gamblers to the fact that they were under observation so I had to reserve our services beyond a real safety point. I've been able to infiltrate the usual observers and students but they've had no proper back-up forces. I'd have come myself before now but I couldn't take the risk of being recognized by Euri."

"And now it's too late," Euri said with relief. "Eternity is almost here and your staff will be occupied with their own problems."

Blue's body was dragged out without ceremony: its arms and legs, comically independent of an owner who owned them no longer, seemed anxious to be off and away as they dangled and snatched at obstructions and tripped the attendants. Equally obstreperous, the survivors of earlier Games were now forcing their way through the crowd to reach vantage points near the Cube. The crowd resisted at a distance but when they came close, still proudly wearing their red or blue masks, the crowd shrank back in dismay.

The hastily patched bodies of the survivors looked on the point of coming apart and the only living thing in them was the euphoric drug they'd been injected with: it glowed in their eyes, crawled beneath the skin, jerked the limbs impatiently and made the air round them sickly with its breath. Even if these bodies kept going till Midnight was there any living soul in them to enjoy Eternity or would the drug usurp their rights?

"I should have quarantined this place long ago," Bubo cried out, trembling and unconscious of the crowd that glared suspiciously. "It's my fault: I should never have sent brave but inexperienced men in here. Do you know who the man you killed was?" he said, turning towards Euri with the air of one who speaks of the sublime simplicities above questions of good or bad taste. "He was a young Social Welfarer I sent to play the Game with you, so that he could observe you with your psychosocial barriers down. It was a drastic step but I had had such difficulty in getting through to you, in finding out what lay at the bottom of all your problems. He volunteered, it's true, but if I had *known*—and I ought to have known. . . . Of course, as soon as the news of the tragic accident was received, I organized a rescue operation but your friends, the Gamblers, with all the cunning of the sick, had concealed the body and though I maintained the search long after all possibility of revival was gone I had to call off the search. I can't condemn myself enough: timing is everything and I was too late. It was a very serious error. . . ."

"I killed your *spy*?"

"Don't you see how your very vocabulary shows your imbalance? I should never have recommended you for work at the History Academy."

"What a mess you've made!" Leni cried. "I shall report all this to the Press Academy."

"Inform against your own husband?" Chrys said.

"Professional loyalty is higher than marital," Bubo said with a look of surprised gratitude. "In fact, the Press Academy was cleared last night before the experiment was undertaken. They agreed that there was no useful purpose to be served in publicizing something so atypical of our society and lacking in general interest."

"Will I ever be free of you?" Euri whispered.

Bubo turned apologetically to him: "I accept all responsibility. You were not to know—how could you?—that the experiment would turn out so disastrously. And society owes you so much already."

"Don't you understand that your experiment has made me a murderer, a *fugitive*?"

No wonder the dead man pursued him, not accepting the bargain the Gamblers made with each other!

"You are *not* a 'murderer'—any more than you're a 'peasant' or a 'scullion' or a 'lawyer' or a 'policeman'. You are not to blame. You are *our* symptom and as such you perform a vitally important role: without you we cannot know what our diseases are."

"And what of the man I killed?"

"Why, nothing. His affairs were wound up within minutes of his officially certified relinquishment, as is usual. He had no close relatives or friends, otherwise he would not have been accepted as a volunteer. I recorded his eulogy while I was waiting for you this morning. I spoke of him as a Welfarer who had voyaged through the bloody seas of men's hearts—nothing *personal* intended, of course, Euri!—and not returned. . . . His colleagues had a collection for him this morning—all the usual decencies have been observed."

"But is he owed nothing?" Euri said, relieved despite himself by Bubo's official exorcism of the dead man.

"How can the non-existent be owed anything? How can we make the dead the creditors of the living? In his life he was happy and successful. He had brilliant hopes that will never be disappointed now. But the dead do not concern us: it is the living we must protect. In one of those archaic expressions you so admire, it is *you* who are the 'victim-survivor' of the catastrophe. You can have no conception of how I suffered as I watched you this morning struggling with fear-induced mirages. My colleagues demanded that you be requested to ask for surgery before you infected everyone around you, but I maintained that a lasting cure could only come from voluntary action.

"I waited all day with dwindling hopes, and I was on the verge of giving up when you made your first tentative gropings towards help by asking me to come here. . . ."

Euri interrupted him savagely: "Will you play the Game with me?"

He did not anticipate Bubo's reaction. After a quick glance at Chrys, Bubo nodded agreement without the least surprise.

"Are you going mad as well?" Leni cried. "Midnight is only two watches away!"

"I owe Euri this."

It was obvious that Euri, long past rational thought, wanted to kill his Servant. The two women clung to them and tried to prevent their leaving but the crowd, once it had understood what the issue was, joined wholeheartedly into the struggle: Chrys and Leni were torn away from the two men. Euri took Bubo to the Judge and made formal application.

Bubo took the blue mask, Euri the red, and stripping off their looser clothing and removing their shoes they took their place in the queue. Here they could not see the Game but only hear the cries and groans of the audience, knowing that groans meant a missed opportunity and laughter and applause a hit that had crushed bone and muscle. Euri watched Bubo from behind his mask—Bubo disdainfully refused to wear his before entering the Cube—and he was astonished how unaffected Bubo was by the sordid scene. He envied the Servant's training that enabled him to adapt so quickly—but soon another thought began to trouble him: he remembered Bubo's look at Chrys and knew that not only he was menaced by Bubo. Had the Servant all along determined to engineer his death so that he would never enter Eternity?

At last they were called. From inside the Cube, Euri saw the faces of the crowd, like so many expressionless lumps of clay waiting for him and Bubo to infuse them with life. He must not direct his hate against *them*.

Bubo won the ball. Euri saw this as a bad omen. By now he believed that nothing had been left to chance. The blue mask concealed Bubo's mild and benevolent expression and revealed a compact, powerful, predatory animal. But the Servant's first throw restored Euri to sanity. Unused to the heft of a ball ten times as heavy as the one normally used in the Ballgame, Bubo threw wild. Euri stood and watched the silver ball hit the dead floor after two passes that came nowhere near either of them. The crowd jeered faintly and faraway through the glass wall and Bubo looked round in apparent surprise. Euri picked up the ball and aimed an elementary shot to rebound at Bubo's legs. The Servant's obvious inexperience had disarmed him of his hate: he couldn't kill an inferior.

Bubo eluded that shot with ease. He recovered the ball where it lay at his feet and returned it with surprising accuracy, waist high. Euri's reflexes took him out of danger. He began to play with an icy determination but, despite his experience, he found the Servant with his intelligence and well-trained reflexes not so inferior a match after all. He dodged all Euri's standard shots—not so difficult a matter if the direction and spin of the ball as it left the other player's hand were well judged, for the path of the ball after it hit the side of the Cube was entirely predictable—and Euri soon regretted that he had abandoned the initiative in that first shot.

The pace of the Game soon tired them. The crowd fell silent as the contest continued long past the time others had taken. Euri's body grew sluggish and failed to respond to his commands. Bubo had surprised him by his rapid grasp of the tactical possibilities of the present situation: once he had rebounded the ball from where Chrys's face was pressed against the glass and another time from the terrifying broken face of one of the survivors who was breathing with the aid of an accordion pump.

He began to hear from his body the first suggestion of the fatalism which was the main danger of the Game: however weary the body became the walls never lost energy. However weakly thrown, the ball returned always at the same dazzling speed, so that to the tiring mind of the Gambler it seemed the returns came harder and that the Cube absorbed his energy and turned it against him. Euri's reflexes were becoming more and more erratic and he thought with dismay that soon only his will, that clumsy rider, would be in control. He was sweat-drenched, suffocating, hardly able to see Bubo for the salt that ran into his stinging eyes.

A shock and a tearing pain along his right arm told him that he'd been hit. He couldn't distinguish hand or fingers in the pain. Off-balance, the crowd like hounds in the distance, he saw the brilliant triumph that shone on the blue mask.

Not thinking or judging, a slotmachine responding in the only way it was capable of, Euri swung round, scooped the ball clumsily with his left hand and, as if collapsing, shielded his throw from Bubo with his body and threw himself forward with all his weight in the hurtling ball, lengthening himself on the floor as the ball flashed back over his prone body. He heard the blow on Bubo's frame and his heart missed a beat. He knew it was a shock to stop the pulse of any being. He twisted round where he lay and saw Bubo on his back, oddly folded, in the far corner where the strike had thrown him.

Euri was too exhausted to get up. He lay listening to the wild, distant applause. He wondered where Chrys had got to but he had no energy for emotions. It occurred to him that the debt society owed him must now be enormous. A Servant-killer! He felt almost sorry that Eternity would come before he would have a chance to enjoy compensation.

The Servant's body was dragged out of the Cube at the end of a chain. As Euri followed it out into the freezing air of the vaulted hall he saw that it was steaming. The crowd laughed uproariously at him in complicity. Was he free? Bubo's mask had fallen off and on the face was an open-mouthed gape of surprise. It satisfied Euri to have been able to deal out that surprise. When the body had been taken to the Viewing-Room, he showered, had his clothes laundered and his arm treated. The nerve had been numbed and there was some extensive bruising which was soon put right.

He went to the Viewing-Room. Chrys and Leni were there. He detected groping at his heart the death-wish conscience that would soon attack in strength—but first it had to sound his defences, learn his weakpoints, infiltrate his rearguard so that when its main assault came in wave upon wave of guilt, remorse, horror, self-disgust, it would know where best to strike. He suddenly remembered the white-coated pleasantly-smiling man who had interviewed him when he applied for Deprived Child Status and stained his hands with red Rorschach blots: *Explain! Explain!*

He looked at his chronometer. The 11th watch! He'd hoped to disentangle some of the threads of his life before Eternity came with its all-revealing light. . . .

Leni was guarding her husband's body. Seeing Euri, she said contemptuously: "I've called for assistance. He's suffered little structural damage, I think, and is only in a state of shock-suspense. He can be easily revived. Don't imagine you've harmed him."

"You can't get assistance here. Didn't you understand we were playing for Life and Death? There's no way of getting help from outside in time to prevent his death becoming incurable."

"Servants and criticos go nowhere incognito. A rescue force was despatched as soon as it was known where we were going and has been in touch with me for the past five minutes. An abandonment of Servant-status is a serious matter! Any minute now Social Maintenance will be here. Our last duty will be to disinfect this place—it should have been done long ago. I'm not sure what Bubo intended. Possibly he wanted you to re-enact the accident of last night. We shall know when he's revived. If it weren't for Liberation you'd have seen an adaptation of this episode on TV. I happen to know that my husband was making you the subject of his doctoral thesis."

"I thought I was only to be Appendix A."

As Euri stood thinking, a giant voice startlingly filled the immense hall. "This is Social Maintenance! Please assist us by co-operating. You are in grave psychosocial danger. Our instructions are to offer you every assistance. We are required to remind you of your Constitutional right to refuse medical aid: this right is temporarily waived by Congressional Order 7432794 of today's date, watch 23.01. This is . . ."

"Liberation is in less than an hour!" Euri cried. "What are you hoping to do?"

"The less time, the more urgency. We'll continue to do our duty until the last micro-second," Leni replied proudly.

At this moment a chemical light-bomb exploded and exposed the vast emptiness of the Space Museum, shooting out shrapnel light-bullets that ricochetted off cylinders and cantilevered arms that had perhaps shone as nakedly in space. The light-bullets flared in every dark corner like stars. Euri was so terrified by the *expression* that flashed from the space monsters that he hardly noticed the armoured mobile observation-rooms, packed with medico-technicians, that raced across the floor towards the crowd and the Cube, waving their sensors, atmospheric samplers,

TV eyestalks writhing ecstatically. The awful *brxzz-brxzz* of the psycho-emergency alarm brought him back to reality. Behind the observation-rooms a brigade of medi-commandos were advancing with rocket-assisted leaps, firing their tranquillizer-dart machine-pistols.

The crowd dispersed and fled in all directions, but many went down in the first discharge of darts. A jelly-bomb exploded over the Cube and covered it with a foam that set hard in a second, trapping the players inside. Sleeping-gas bombs puffed pinkly over the floor. In an ordinary building the rescuers would by now have swept all before them but they were not used to such unprecedented conditions. Euri heard the amplified voice choke at the horror of this scene of psychosocial disaster and beg the fleeing people not to bring down on themselves the shameful epithet *refugee.* With the two women and Bubo's corpse he had been hidden from the rescuers by the screens of the Viewing-Room, but now Leni ran out to call for attention.

Euri grabbed Chrys's hand and together they raced towards the back of the Museum, into the far darkness, keeping under cover as best they could, Chrys as eager as he was to escape. They didn't get far before they were overtaken by a mobile searchlight. Euri pulled Chrys to a halt and they remained motionless until the searchlight—a limited machine that knew only to follow suspicious movement—having bobbed round in its search-pattern, its war dance, raced back to where the excitement was.

They rested for a few moments. The rescuers had their hands full elsewhere. Only Euri and Chrys had dared come this way. Darkness was not a familiar or friendly experience for Magellanites. Most of those who'd fled were now returning and greeting the medicos and the Social Maintenancemen with cries of relief. A long line of panic-sacked stretcher-cases which was moving rapidly out of the Museum to be flown off in ambulances was jostled by volunteers who'd seen the disaster on TV: Servants, students, creative writers, criticos, Congressional Vice-Presidents, ministers of religion distributing application forms.

It was time to get out of the building. Soon Social Maintenance would have the entire Museum under quarantine. Euri led the way further into the darkness, determined to evade capture until Liberation rescued him. Where he was going was actually the old front of the Museum. The entrance which the Gamblers and the rescuers had used was at the back service area, and he felt sure that there must be plenty of exits in the other direction. It was unlikely that Social Maintenance had the entire building under guard. Their techniques were leisurely and infallible under normal conditions. In twenty-four hours they could extend their assistance to every cranny and corner of the world. Now they had less than an hour. Even so it was not easy for the two to overcome the knowledge of a lifetime and believe that they could successfully reject help. Euri breathed over and over to himself: *Liberation!*

Their footsteps sounded louder as the commotion behind them was calmed. They had no time to lose. They moved cautiously in the darkness through corridors, around balconies and along ramps. The designers of the building had had an insane sense of theatre and Euri, forced to flash his lamp dangerously more than once to avoid tumbling into some ornamental abyss, cursed them viciously. He was surprised to hear Chrys laughing quietly as he did so.

The Gamblers themselves hadn't cared to investigate the interior of the Museum where all was dust and decay and the showcases contained lumps of rock picked off barren worlds that might, or might not, contain fossil spores; or that had markings that could, but might not, have been made by intelligent creatures; photographs that no one had ever been able to decipher but that no one had ever been able to prove were faked; peculiar, possibly significant, radar readings that might be confirmed, one day, as the first evidence of extraterrestial life—hopes that were in themselves, as any modern medico could have told them, psychological disasters to entertain. They came to a room where huge globes of planets and moons hung from the ceiling. Some had crashed to the floor and Euri and Chrys ran their hands over the rough surfaces, the mountains and valleys of these worlds. Eternity. Euri checked his chronometer again. Only half a watch left of this life! He took a tighter hold of Chrys and hurried her on but she tugged at his arm and said: "What's that?" pointing to a dimly glowing rectangle at the end of a corridor leading from the room.

"It's a window, thank God."

Closer, they felt the cold night air and saw vaguely through the glass that the years had made almost opaque the red glow of Magellan's celebrations. They *had* to get back there before Midnight. Euri kicked the glass out. They heard it smashing just outside, so it was a short drop to the ground.

They scrambled out. Even the dank air of the Old City smelled good after the musty Museum. The moon shone down but could cast no shadows on the glare that was Magellan. They were on a wide curving ramp that led down towards a ditch through the ruins—a maintenance road. There was no sign of activity on the road or anywhere this side of the Museum. They saw an ambulance hurtle overhead and they began to run towards Magellan, hardly speaking, so intent were they on the gigantic crackling and hissing that filled the air, the irregular hammer pulse, the rockets that flared across the sky as Magellan consumed itself. Euri felt a wild excitement. Whatever happened the world could never be the same again.

They did not stop running until they were sure they weren't being pursued, but long before that they were exhausted. The road was rough and full of small, treacherous obstacles, never having been intended for walking. Behind them the Space Museum parodied and mocked in its thousand black windows the celebrations of Magellan.

Not much further along the road, Euri recognized a familiar ruin and leading Chrys over the top of it came to a station not far down the line from where they had left the flier. He called it, though taking a chance that Social Maintenance would have traced it through Leni and deputized it, and was glad to see it arrive unaccompanied a few seconds later. They got in and ordered it to Congress Plaza. It seemed to know nothing of the affair at the Space Museum. They saw with relief the ruins of the Old City fly backwards and rejoiced when they leaped from the surface rails and swam once more in the light of Magellan.

Apologizing at full volume, the flier put them down some distance from the Plaza on the outskirts of the enormous crowd, spouting statistics of previous New Year's Eve crowds in the eternal self-justification of machinery. They left it and pushed through the crowd. The canal had stopped flowing but the surface erupted in small sprays of platelets from time to time where the current tried to find a way through. The air was full of a red fog of smoke and incense.

As they entered the crowd a single deer came scattering madly out, red eyes rolled backwards, foam around its jaws. Further in they came across other animals lying dead underfoot and even one or two people were sprawling, their bodies trampled into and half submerged beneath the surface of the canal. Euri took Chrys by the arm and pushed deeper into the crowd, through an inertia more infuriating than any active resistance. Many had torn clothes and looked dazed, some had blue or deathly grey faces and dark-ringed eyes. They stared at the sky in mirrors or TV's. Euri heard Chrys's sharp note of horror at the sight of some mutilated, trembling creature replied to by the crowd with strange other-worldly cries. He wished with all his soul that it was morning again.

Darkness! The rockets had stopped and all the lights faded and were gone. There was a sudden painful pressure in the ears that was silence. There was no sound except for a few isolated screams and laughs that measured the extent of the crowd. And on the wall of the night the monstrous, fiery figures 23:59:00 . . 01 . . 02. . . .

In the silence they heard faintly the haunting wind sweeping away the acrid, gritty incense clouds. . . .

23:59:48

Chimes began to toll out the old world and the world responded—

One—no more uncertain. . . . *Two*—how weak we were! . . . *Three* for no more masters. . . . *Four*—come out of hiding. . . . *Five* is for real. . . . *Six* and no one loved me. . . . *Seven* never loss again. . . . *Eight* you cannot harm me. . . . *Nine, Ten, Eleven! Break the prison-house!*

At *Twelve* dies Death!

For a moment Euri thought he saw a gigantic mocking face fill the heavens but this vanished as the world erupted and swept him away from Chrys. He fought helplessly against the surging, irresistible crowd, gone mad, a flood with no regard for individual desires that sprang through the streets like a terribly purposeful animal. There was a universal scream of disappointment. Every man was struck blind and lashed out, and as his blows landed opened new eyes, red and glaring, on those he destroyed.

Liberation!

A bitter despair gripped Euri. He struck out in savage rage but all his energies were needed to prevent his being trampled under the crowd. Miraculously, he preserved his balance. What had happened? Where was Chrys? He shouted her name but could hardly hear himself in that raging human storm.

Magellan still stood! Its towers still hung over him—it still imprisoned him in its walls. Nothing had changed. He felt no sense of power, no sense of unlimited reach or immortality. He was only conscious of weakness and constriction, alone in a world that did not expand but instead closed in on him. He had been cheated. Had it all been an experiment by the Servants, like that performed on himself by Bubo but on a world scale? Had Chronophage gone rogue? The terrible disillusionment poisoned his will: all he could think of was to find Chrys.

At last he divined the direction the crowd was taking him in and fought his way out of it. Where was the promised land? Where were his magic powers? Finally, the howling current of humanity swung away and left him stranded but taking Chrys with it. Now he was safe on the outside he turned and followed the crowd. Soon it began to split and then break up into smaller crowds and groups but in none of them could he see Chrys. He needed no more proof than Chrys's disappearance that Liberation had failed. He followed every large group until it disintegrated into fleeing individuals, passing through every street in Magellan until at last he found himself on the canal that circled Magellan, and still no sign of her. Too exhausted to continue, he lay down in the middle of the canal that was still moving sluggishly round the city and let it carry him along while he tried desperately to think.

The towers of Magellan were dark: there was not a light to be seen anywhere. The sky was dark and the moon gone behind it. At the centre of his being a whirlpool sucked away all thought before it became coherent. Where was Chrys? Why had Liberation not come? He completed almost a quarter circuit of the city before he came back to life, jumped to his feet and began to run back towards his apartment. Magellan seemed almost devoid of life, the towers no longer sang with energy. What held them up now? The canals flowed more slowly and in some streets only rocked and lapped with sullen hissing against the steps and walls of buildings. He saw only a few hurrying secret figures, no one he recognized, no Servants, no one to tell him what was happening. The TV either didn't respond or showed mysterious shadows which he switched off in terror.

Despite a weariness, like a hand on his shoulder pulling him down, he was determined to get back to the apartment, the only place he could hope to find Chrys. He wondered why he had taken the promise of Eternity seriously. He despised himself, alone and weak, lost, disorientated—

nothing here that corresponded with omnipotence.

He had not understood how big Magellan was when he had ridden the streets so swiftly. Now he saw dark entrances and alleys he had never seen before. As he struggled along, it seemed to him that the city had in dying imposed its own slow time on him. When, after many hours, he reached his apartment tower at last he felt utterly insignificant. The gondola carried him up the side of the building erratically, as if it too were corrupted. He thought it was going to let go and fall from the wall. How would he get out of his apartment again if the machines failed? If the machines came completely to a stop humanity was done for. But his chronometer said Midnight plus four and still prayed for him.

At long last the gondola clambered to the fortieth floor. He jumped out and stood on the balcony. No sign of light or life inside. He knew that Chrys had not returned. He felt as if his air supply had been cut off. What could have happened to her? What could have prevented her from returning?

He looked out over Magellan. Everywhere the familiar landmarks still stood—but now indistinguishable from the Old City, black hulks against the dark sky. His heart slowed as he felt the death of the city creep into his very bones. There had never been a single minute since he had opened his eyes on the world that Magellan had not blazed with light. Now there was no light; and worse than that—even more fundamental a loss for it had penetrated body and mind, awake or asleep, and set the rhythm of his heartbeats—the pulse of the city was quieted and there was nothing but the desultory sounds of the wind and the creaking building, shrinking in the cold.

The TV no longer listened to his commands. He had to find the join in the wall, jam his fingers in and pull it open. Fortunately, there was no power to lock it. He went inside but didn't need to look to know that she wasn't there. The room was like ice. He shivered, longing for warmth, but the room grew colder visibly—it grew steely and hostile.

There was something strange about it—it struck him with an eerie thrill that it was far colder in the apartment than it was outside. That could not be right. Even if the room could no longer manufacture heat its temperature should only drop after some hours to that of the night air. He couldn't be sure, because his only experience of unscientific conditions had been in the ruins of the Old City. The room mocked his misery. He shuddered and spun round to face the window.

The knowledge of the truth came to him at last without the exhilaration he had anticipated. *Liberation.* At Midnight Liberation had come just as it had been promised. The room, Magellan itself, the entire world now conformed to the geography of his soul. He understood now his disappointment and despair. Not once had he made a wish, a *command.* He had waited for Heaven to reveal itself and, nothing happening, night and hopes had grown darker.

He had to take a grip on the situation—if only he had held tight to Chrys and had faith in himself he need never have plunged into this ocean of misery, cold room, cold heart. He had only to make a wish.

His heartbeats rattled staccato. The night was full of unseen presences that waited for him to make the irrevocable wish. He turned slowly to allow whatever was behind him to wriggle out of sight. He took hold of himself. He hesitated, trying to think of the smallest possible wish, and then as deliberately as he could he willed the room to become warmer. At first nothing happened but after a time it became perceptibly less cold and, as his confidence increased, warmth and light came flooding back into the room.

But the warmth and light caused him to wonder why he had lost Chrys; why he had returned alone to the apartment; why Magellan still stood—he had thought that his hatreds and desires would have swept the city out of existence.

The room grew colder again as it copied his mood. He made it warmer again but it was to be tedious work if he had consciously to will at every moment the conditions he required. Before he could accomplish anything he had to learn the rules of living in Eternity—and he'd thought there were to be no more laws!

He sat down in his chair and remembered what he had been told about Chronophage. The brain was capable of receiving his thoughts, correcting and amplifying his crude visualizations with its vast reservoir of knowledge and synthesizing what he wanted in a millisecond from the surrounding atoms. He decided to make some small experiments. What could he ask for? 'An 'apple'? He held out his hand palm upward and before he had even consciously worded his request an apple appeared on it. He started and found himself clutching it like a madman. He opened his fingers eagerly and examined the apple minutely. It was as heavy and real as anything in his experience—impossible to believe that it had just appeared from out of the air! Yet he had certainly never seen an apple before and had had only a general idea of what it ought to be like, having always suspected it to be a mythical fruit that had never actually existed—but then it was not necessary for it to have existed: anything was possible now—apples or dragons!

He ate the apple. It had an altogether new and fresh taste. The implications of his powers bewildered him. He need not eat at all if Chronophage preserved his body for him the way he saw himself and supplied all the energy he could use. Not needing to eat—or sleep?—would leave all his time for more important things.

To his surprise the centre of the apple turned out to be hard and uneatable. He held it well away from him and ordered it to disappear. It gave no sign of vanishing. He threw it on to the floor and willed it to go until he made his head ache, but it lay there as solid as ever. Words were of no avail. He couldn't make it disappear from his mind: thinking kept it in being however loud his commands. Presumably it would evaporate into its constituent atoms only when he forgot about it. He kicked it into a corner. At this moment he was more interested in his powers of creation than those of destruction. Why hadn't he been trained to understand the ways of Eternity? How long was it going to take him to find Chrys?

Now it dawned on him that he had no idea how much of the city or his apartment was the residue of prior 'reality' and what was the new creation of his omnipotence. He walked round the room, stamping on the floor, weighing everything he could lift—all seemed equally substantial. He fixed his attention on his old chair and changed its shape and colour but as soon as he turned away it seemed to return with alacrity to its old form. His knowledge of the chair as it had always been was stronger than his new conception of it. An entirely new chair proved easy enough to create and maintain in being but it seemed that to succeed in changing the old one permanently he would have to lose his grasp of what he thought of as reality. In time he might be able to create and dismiss things at will but if he insisted on the solidity of the world—and he couldn't imagine an Eternity passed in a dream—it called for mental powers he could hardly believe possible.

He created duplicates of the TV and the other machines in the room and couldn't tell which was old and which was new. Old or new, the TV's brought him no message from the outside world. He re-created Chrys's sculptures but they were more sullen than ever. He soon realized that he was wasting time with all these creation exercises—evading the real problem. Since all his needs were supplied there was no point in making machines, food, drink or clothing. All these things were unnecessary and distracted him from the only action his new powers made significant—the creation of a new world.

He had created dead things, mechanical things: could he create life? Insects?—those little machines were hardly life as he thought of it. He created a mouse—it wriggled in his hand and looked at him with brilliant little eyes. He uttered a shout of surprise and dropped it. Before he could check it it had run under a bookcase and vanished. He didn't repeat the experiment.

His own face and body—the being he had so long felt not to be his real self—he left untouched. He needed for the time being some touchstone of the former world—and how would Chrys recognize him if he changed?

Where could Chrys be? How had she solved the problems of Liberation?

He tried the TV once again but there was no response

from that once infallible oracle. He tried to analyse the effect his emotions, unconscious desires, memories, incorrect vizualizations might have on Chrys but he felt his control over the world leaving him long before he could come to any conclusion. Had she deliberately abandoned him—or had he abandoned her? He called her name softly but she didn't come. It was very quiet and still. Not a sound came from the city outside.

He shut his eyes and tried to picture her sitting opposite him. Everything he had forgotten about her appearance was like a betrayal. At last he dared open his eyes. Something sat in the other chair. It was still and shadowed, lifeless. Terror gripped him and he screamed at it to leave him alone. He couldn't move. He buried his head in his arms for some minutes but he had to look—the ghost, whatever it was that had responded to his call, still waited for him to acknowledge it. He wished it had taken its chance of life like the mouse and run. For an age he sat, sick at heart, sure that Chrys was dead. The shadow slowly faded from the room.

He remembered at long last that it was impossible to die in Eternity. Whatever happened in this world Chrys had some existence somewhere. One thing was certain: he would never again attempt to drag her from where she was. If she would not come for him he must go and look for her.

There was no sign of the dawn. From the balcony the streets looked as empty as before. Chrys was somewhere out there—or perhaps somewhere where the sun was shining and flowers and fruits grew in the open air and Magellan was only a memory. He began to feel the night chill invade the room again. It was impossible for him to create his paradise until he found her.

Looking for any clue he went into the smaller room . . . *the sunlit dormitory of his earliest memory . . . the future evaporating like a nightmare. . . .* He threw himself backwards through the door, having nearly been trapped in childhood, his heart thumping wildly. What would have happened if he'd surrendered to that opportunity of escape? Would he have retraced every stage of his life until he came to this moment again . . . and again?

For the second time he experienced a fear such as he'd never known could exist. What other traps lay in wait for him in Eternity? What trap was he in *at this very moment*? He had to learn to cope with this world. He went back to the door and threw it open.

A thousand forgotten things! His old books, TV tapes, his electronic microscope, his portable computer and dial-a-drug—and only the faintest memory of the unhappiness he had also known touched them all with a pleasant sadness. Outside the window the old terrace still stretched, its ornamental trees bent horizontal by the winds that blustered round the 61st floor of the college. The sky was pale blue, just as he always remembered it.

Chronophage had done a good job here. There was no sign of past or future here but only a tranquillity from which the sting of unhappiness and the rage of happiness were equally absent. He sat down at his old desk and again the old dreams that were like so many worlds opening before him. . . .

It seemed to Euri that he had drifted off to sleep. His studies were tedious. He awoke dismayed, something troubling—a play-period missed?—then he remembered that *this* was the dream and dictated to the TV: 'Liberation has arrived. This is Day One 2080. I am only remembering . . ." but then he thought: how can I trust this machine, which is itself only part of the dream, to remind me? He wrote on a piece of paper in luminous ink—the most primitive and solemn medium he knew—the same information, but he understood now that he must rely solely on his intelligence and will and that there was nothing in this world he could rest on.

Why had he returned to this period of his life? Perhaps it was the best stepping-stone into Eternity. At this time there were a thousand roads for him to follow—there was no end to the future! The sun shone through the window, stationary, eternal. His books suggested that he might be a hundred different men with a hundred different futures and none of them to end up with the History Academy or Chrys. It was the thought of Chrys that brought him back. Even so it was with a terrible sense of claustrophobia, a desperate struggle of the will, that he forced himself through the ever-narrowing future, denied the thousand worlds and emerged again in 2080 and—he laughed sadly—Eternity.

He left his college room, not daring to look back, and deliberately walked through the wall to assert his control: the wall faded, dissolved and parted round him and he found himself once again in his apartment.

The room was unchanged. Behind him, the closed door of the other room. Outside, Magellan, dark as ever. A long and dark night!

But how long had he spent in the dream? His chronometer still said Midnight plus four. The timeless quality of existence frightened him: he had no way of knowing how long had actually passed. Had *years*—he'd better say *Earth orbits of the Sun*—passed while he'd dreamed in his college room? Had Chrys come and seen the empty apartment and left long ago? If only he could grasp the logic of Eternity. Could he return to the actual moment of his return here?—move freely back and forth in Eternity, stepping from Time to Time as on stepping-stones in a river? Or was his concept of Time meaningless in Eternity, and here a different structure connected him with Chrys—or was there no structure at all? No wonder he had tried to flee Eternity!

As far as he could see no one else inhabited his Eternity. There might be only an infinitely small chance of clashing with another's Eternity. He might be living at the speed of his thoughts and all this have taken place seconds after Midnight. Magellan might still be a blaze of light and warmth to others. Or a hundred years might have passed and all the others long since departed to explore their infinite worlds and he alone, chained by old desires, hardly begun.

He went out on to the balcony and stood looking out over the city for some time. No sign of the dawn, and when he checked his chronometer he found—not altogether to his surprise—that the time had advanced by not a single minute. He gathered his resolution and commanded the morning.

The sky lightened, a fire kindled on the eastern horizon and the sun rose and threw long golden rays through the city—Magellan lay quietly in the morning light. Euri swayed and clutched at the balcony rail as he felt the awful tug of vertigo. He looked down at the streets but could see no sign of people or animals. He looked up at the sun in wonder. He felt small—the only survivor of his self-destruction.

He watched the city in anticipation, not knowing that he was waiting for an omen. Soon there appeared in the sky, high above the horizon, a few specks like spots on a TV screen, so that momentarily he thought his world was disintegrating, going out of focus. The spots grew larger, spread out and then jumped out of the screen at him, a flock of birds, chattering to each other, oblivious of him.

Elated, knowing beyond doubt that they were real and the harbingers of others to come, he shouted a welcome to them but they sailed over him on the wind, unaware of him. How he valued their indifference and freedom from his commands. If only he were as free!

He stretched out his arms wide and wider. They curved and broadened and became covered with blade-like feathers. He rose from the balcony and floated, the building drifting away behind him. Ponderously flapping his new and heavy wings he ascended into the sky. When he was high enough to see the Plaza, Congress and the Academies that surrounded it he commenced a long glide between the peaks of Magellan. The city turned and aligned itself to him. He had expected a confidence-crisis once he was in mid-space but now he felt that his knowledge of his world was complete.

It was not long, however, before he realized that he owed to Chronophage all his powers of levitation and that he was not really flying, not being supported by the air his wings displaced. He wanted to soar, to follow the beautiful, inevitable, *free* curves that the birds traced like skaters on the sky. As he sank he worked his wings regularly up and down.

He was not succeeding in the slightest in flying like a bird. His wings were an encumbrance to him and pulled him down like heavy clothing in water. He leaned more steeply against the air, called up a stronger wind against himself, but he only began to topple slowly head over heels, wrongly shaped, wrongly balanced, wrongly proportioned. If he dared submit completely to Nature he knew he would drop like a stone: without submitting he could not learn to fly. Yet learning meant to be shaped by the air into bird form—to fly was to be a bird—and he was afraid to lose his human shape.

He settled down towards ground level, bitterly disappointed that he had not experienced the shaping air, the interbalance of forces, the floating curve of a bird's path. He sank precisely to where he wanted to be and stood once more on the canal. His arms he returned to normal.

The canal no longer flowed. It was overgrown with bright red fragile growth and everything on its banks was decayed and rusted. Notices and street signs were fallen and swivelled and could no longer be relied on. Shops were dusty and empty: the air curtains that had protected them were no longer blowing and the wind lounged in aimlessly and unchecked.

He walked towards Congress Plaza, looking for any sign of life. It was still and quiet as if a plague had fallen on the city. Once he thought he saw a patch of furry hide through a cluster of signposts and antennae but it vanished when he turned to look at it and he hurried on. He saw no sign of animals apart from that. Some brambles that were growing up a broad flight of steps bearing black and green berries were untouched. A small tree was growing through the concrete of a landing pier and all round it were fallen, uneaten fruits. He saw that many of the towers were covered with a creeper from which hung branches of green leaves and white flowers. One creeper had reached the fiftieth storey. How long could it have taken these plants to grow? He gasped with terror at the thought of the Time that had escaped him, and rushed on through the silent, unmoving streets until he reached the Plaza.

He looked round over its wide expanse. Little had changed, though the History Academy was looking ricketier than ever and the searchlight eyes of Magellan's statue no longer shone—that gaze had turned inwards. Congress Dome still floated there. If anything of the Universal Society still existed it must have its headquarters there. As he got closer he was excited to see a small and obviously makeshift sign: *Registration and Assistance Commission.* The sudden hope this aroused made him run all the way to the entrance: perhaps he could get news of Chrys.

There was no TV at the door to welcome him and tell him what was going on. He walked through the familiar door: everything was so desolate that he was amazed to find thousands of people sitting silent and watchful inside in a darkness that was hardly relieved at all by a number of primitive lamps scattered over the floor. The old fittings were gone and now there was only a huge bare space in which people squatted or covered their heads and lay curled in sleep as if they didn't expect early attention. There were tables covered with newspapers and pamphlets. Groups of backs turned out to be gathered round TV screens: as he went eagerly to join them they all turned to stare at him, then returned to the TV with looks of disappointed contempt. He had expected to be glad to see his fellow men again but now that he was with them he felt no interest. These people were nothing but refugees and there was no possibility they could help him.

He pushed his way through the crowd and watched the TV for a while with intense interest but the screen showed nothing but contorted faces, close-ups of noses and ears, a bloodshot eye filled the screen and the crowd shrank back. A jangle of what sounded and looked like a thousand people calling for attention made Euri's eyes and ears ache. He wondered where the transmission was coming from until a large blob resolved itself into his own face staring blankly from the screen and he wondered no longer. He moved to go and was immediately hustled away by the crowd.

With what different hopes he had last attended Congress!

These people—he felt less certain than he had about the birds that these were real and not just poor imitations that Chronophage had found its mind populated with. Where were the signatures of omnipotence and immortality—purpose, joyousness? These were timid and anxious; they looked eagerly at him, trying to catch his eye, and then nervously away again when he saw them, but edging closer to him each time. He heard their never-ceasing stream of complaints—where were the masseur-psychiatrists?—the mobile voting-booths? Some said they couldn't recall when they'd last been asked to vote. They snapped their golden-tipped fingers, tossed their long waved hair and smoothed silken overalls over plump thighs.

Some furtively created small luxuries and vanished them again, fearful of losing their right to assistance. Euri saw with disgust the situation he had allowed himself to fall into but while there was any chance at all of getting news of Chrys he had to restrain himself.

The newspapers and pamphlets were of no more help to him. There was no concrete news in them but only long well-reasoned appeals to show loyalty to the Universal Society and vague warnings of what had happened to those who had disappeared. There were hundreds of pages of personal ads: heartrending appeals in short rhyming poems to husbands, wives, lovers, sons and daughters. The paper in his hand was dog-eared, dirty and the print faded and grey from much reading. He threw it down and hurried off, not knowing where to go or how to get some genuine advice. As he paused, undetermined, a bell rang and a man who had been sleeping jumped to his feet and ran towards an inner door, followed by a hundred envious glances. How had he known the bell was for him?

"When your turn comes you will know," said a polite young man, who looked at Euri understandingly. He was neatly and inconspicuously dressed. Euri had not seen him approach. At this moment there was a diversion—the young man, the crowd and Euri himself all turned to watch an obvious official who now crossed the room, a sheaf of papers rustling and quivering irritably in his hand. He was dressed in grey clerical overalls with gold hoops round his cap which indicated—was it possible?—seven hundred years Incorruptibility. His eyes were grey mirrors. Euri thought the official looked pleased to see him but when he caught his eye he looked down and disappeared through a door in a temporary partition.

The politeness of the polite young man was a positive reproach to Euri, who felt obliged to make some remark. He noticed without much surprise that the young man's appearance had altered until now he could almost have been taken as Euri's younger brother—a gesture of respect, the young man indicated modestly when he saw that Euri had recognized himself. Euri wondered what the young man was really like, but the question was meaningless in Eternity. People looked like what they were. The question was what the young man wanted from him.

The young man took from a briefcase he was carrying a picture of a girl and handed it to Euri. This girl was nothing like Chrys: like half the girls in Magellan she looked like a horribly aged—or retarded—version of the current Most Promising Five-Year-Old TV Star. It was a conventional portrait, the girl naked, from the waist up front view, the waist downwards back view, the shoulders sprouting a full face and two profile heads. Euri could see nothing special about it.

"I've spent half Eternity looking for her."

"How can *I* help you?" Euri asked.

"I'm sure you can tell me."

"I don't know her."

"I think you do."

"Why? There's nothing to tell her from millions of other girls. How should I know what distinguishing marks or signals you identify her by? You can surely find plenty of girls like this."

"This one is different."

"Well I don't see how I can help you."

"You are like me."

"Not in a million years!"

"But yes! That's how we've met! That's how things are in Eternity. Like attracts like. You're like me and I'm like you. We both inhabit the same world, don't we? Think of the billions of possible worlds there are in Eternity! It takes more than a slight similarity of fortune to bring us together: *essentially* we're identical, we have the same feelings and needs. That's why we've come together—to help one another."

As the young man spoke he gained confidence and his attitude changed from a modest pathos to cocksureness at the sight of Euri's dismay. His eyes were now on a level with Euri's and his tone had slid down the scale from pleading to threatening. Euri turned his eyes away from that eager face and saw that he was surrounded by gleeful expressions. He was glad he hadn't allowed the other to see what Chrys looked like. The young man took his opportunity to push the photo into Euri's hand and run off, but Euri seized him, struck him and made him take the photo back. The young man collapsed as quickly as he'd grown and became once more a stranger.

At this everyone in the room came rushing, begging advice, exhorting, making menacing gestures apparently in the hope of extorting retaliation, pleading for an exchange of addresses for friendly correspondence. One man held his sleeve and shouted at him in increasing rage as he saw Euri's bewilderment: "Why don't you reply? I'm speaking to you in Gibberish!"

What had Euri to do with these tiny, inefficient desires that were crippled and poisoned by the very thoughts that spawned them? What could he do for them? He had to get away from these creatures before his own purposes were befogged by the mud they stirred up. He beat them off, horrified at seeing watery blue eyes waving on long stalks attracted, insatiable, to anything that moved. Why couldn't they use their powers? What did they want of *him*?

He desperately needed time to think but it seemed as if in Eternity there was no time to stand back and observe one's experiences—to think, to feel *was* to experience.

Just then the bell rang again. Euri clearly heard the personal note in the summons. He pulled himself away from the clawing hands which reluctantly let go only when he made it clear he was intent on entering the other room. He pushed open the tall narrow door, and as he passed through it the tumult of the waiting-room died away. He glanced back and saw his petitioners, clutching the forms and TV tapes on which they had recorded their desires, dirty, crumpled and worn into holes now with long fumbling, hastily returning to their places.

The room he now entered was small and hushed but for a confidential buzz of interview—confession and enquiry, answer and question, explanations of explanations. He had only a minimal hope left that the remains of the Universal Society had any knowledge of his wife but that tiny spark of hope kept him trapped; as his despair increased so his need of Chrys increased and his faith in finding her unaided diminished. The interviews were taking place at a counter divided into compartments in which he could see only the hunched backs of the interviewees. He found an empty compartment and waited for someone to come—but could he expect the trap to explain to him how he was to escape it?

Soon there appeared a large, heavy, stooping man smoking an old-fashioned trombone pipe which he meditatively worked back and forth, his jaw clenched over the mouthpiece. The pipe smoker had fine, sincere eyes and he greeted Euri with every appearance of altruistic satisfaction. Here was someone who could explain things, someone for whom Eternity had no terrors.

"I need a little assistance," Euri began. The other removed his pipe and allowed his face to glow with pleasure.

"Of course," he said. "That's why I'm here."

Euri took comfort from the evident strength of the man. His jaw muscles were developed to the point where they stood out on his cheeks like the chinstrap of a helmet, the helmet itself being the bony dome of head that was divided from his face by heavy eyebrows that joined with a fringe of hair. A face like this would have been in the worst possible taste in the old Magellan but Euri felt glad to see that in Eternity men were no more ashamed of wearing their virtues in public than they had been in primitive times. He began with more hope to attempt an explanation, but before he got two words out the other continued with a calm gentle strength that made Euri's voice seem uncouth and intrusive: "The first question I asked myself immediately after Liberation when I found myself here was: why was I left behind? Now I could easily have complained and demanded a better place since I was certainly promised that Liberation was going to improve my working conditions—I wasn't always as you see me now, Sir!—however, there's never any sense in complaining or whining and I hadn't considered the matter for very long before I realized that the answer to the question why I'd been left here was obvious: *for a very good reason!* I had been put here for a *purpose*. Obviously the authorities think that I can be of most use here. After all, somebody has to do the maintenance work of the world and of Eternity also. You find this a little difficult to understand? Well you would hardly be here if you didn't.

"Let's look at it logically: every action has a cause—everything is therefore inevitable and, being inevitable, *necessary*. What is necessary is *good* and what is good must be gladly accepted and *more* than accepted, *promoted*. . . ."

Euri no longer listened. He thought: how much better I know the things I hate than the things I love! Am I to be *defined* by what I hate? But he determined not to give way entirely to despair, and he broke into the chain of logic with which the pipe smoker was fettering his world and gave him Chrys's full name and description. Even as he spoke he knew his description was utterly inadequate.

The other was not pleased at Euri's interruption. He replaced the pipe in his mouth and allowed a few angry puffs of smoke to escape his lips. At last he said, with an air of stony scrupulosity: "Well, of course we have records here, millions of names and locations, personal details, medical certificates, completed questionnaires—you'll find there's not much about Eternity that we don't know. But is it really worth your time? I'm anxious to help you in any way I can but we must remember that *true* help doesn't always lie in simply giving people what they ask for. The essential point is this: does this girl really exist? Of course I realize she must have some mental existence for you—and that's quite enough certification for Eternity—but did she in fact have any prior medico-legal existence in Magellan? If we can solve this problem we shall be half way to finding her."

"Are you trying to say she's not *real*?" Euri said, so shaken that he wasn't able to be as angry as he'd liked to have been.

"I think that together we ought to examine more closely the first simple and obvious truth that immediately springs to my notice: she's not here. Furthermore, I must tell you that we have received no corresponding approach from any such person as you describe. Now remember, this is Eternity where all our desires and true needs are supplied. I shall put your request before the Committee but in the meantime please consider your position. I ask of you no more than I demand of myself: to face the facts. But don't let me influence you in any way."

Euri shook his head in bewilderment and rage and then he saw that behind the clouds of smoke the other had spouted with every word the counter had become a polished table and the interviewees were now all his interlocutors. He wondered why they thought that a request for assistance gave them the right to question and criticize. Their faces hung dull and heavy with consideration and altruism like overripe fruit, but in the table-top the reflections grimaced and muttered vindictively.

He knew he was losing control. It was like a bad dream. Once he allowed his world to escape him, his dark mind and the malice of other prisoners of Eternity to ally themselves against him, Eternity would be a nightmare from which there was no awakening. But he still clung to the hope that they might have news of Chrys—a hope that was sustained by their very insolence that suggested they had something he wanted.

"Age, height, metabolism?" they asked.

"Twenty-five, 1·77 metres, Melancholic."

"Creativity, ideology, integration?"

"Alpha, Neo-primitive, 35 per cent."

These details—so familiar and beautiful to him—were stuttered out.

The Committee consulted with each other and then looked back at him severely.

"It's not going to be easy to fill such exacting—and, may we say, atavistic—specifications. Nor are they best calculated to promote your psychosocial harmony. Won't you reconsider? . . ."

. The reflected faces jeered at Euri and shouted: *"Pervert!"*

He jumped up and tried to reach them with his fists. He didn't care whether they were only emanations of his guilt-world—that shadowed mirror where his hopes and happinesses were reversed and distorted—or whether they were people such as he might have known in old Magellan: he had to destroy them. As the faces above thc table became outraged and contemptuous, the faces in the table grew more hilariously triumphant. He forced himself to stop and take thought and then conjured into his hand a long iron sword of the kind that was manufactured in vast numbers for the decoration of bachelor apartments. He thrashed away to good effect, sending heads flying like golf-balls, but still, bubbling through the streaming blood, accusations and abuse poured from the lopped-off heads that came rolling rapidly back to him, still jeering. He threw down his sword and ran.

He ran and ran, rebounding from the walls of corridors as if he were in the Cube again. Nobody followed him—perhaps they knew there was no escape. Corridor led into corridor with never an exit. The dull walls seemed a mile thick, a hundred miles thick. But he was becoming familiar with the laws of this world: he knew the walls were thick because he didn't want to return to the streets of Magellan, and he hadn't yet thought what else he wanted to lie outside.

He shut his eyes to see the world he wanted and through his eyelids glowed a wide, free, golden plain. He stepped forward and opened his eyes on the open world. A warm breeze that carried the knowledge of great distances, far places and long-forgotten hopes, stirred his hair. He was truly adrift in Eternity now and if he felt strong and younger than he had ever thought possible as the world stretched without limits before him he also knew that his path was diverging from that of Chrys.

He looked behind him and all round the horizon but there was no trace of Magellan. However, at a short distance, there was a bazaar of tents and stalls and from this came a hullabaloo of laughter. Perhaps the true way to enjoy Eternity was in a tent, never allowing the illusion of stone and steel to impose on life.

Even so his first thought was to strike out into the empty plain and not take the risk of having his dreams contaminated by others as had already happened. He walked briskly off, a thousand paradises in his mind. The plain was empty and the horizon flat, and the wind swept over it a little more coldly than he'd first realized. He knew that no world he could create would give him any pleasure if Chrys was not there to share it. He turned back towards the bazaar, knowing that he had to take any risk to get information since he couldn't conjure Chrys out of his own powers. He walked towards the bazaar thinking that these people might direct him to others and wondering what could be bought and sold in Eternity.

He was aware that his turning back had attracted attention. At his approach two men came eagerly to meet him. They were not an encouraging sight although Euri was by now accustomed to the metamorphoses that had overtaken men in Eternity. One had long legs that slithered over the ground like a frog's, as if he were unable to stand upright. The other had a grey, prematurely wrinkled face over a youth's body. They came up to him smiling confidently.

"Greetings!" the two shouted. "We are agents—Agents Unlimited—we can get you anything you require. Of course you want something—who does not? Come with us, Sir, we have something here we *know* you'll like!"

Curious and unafraid of these ridiculous creatures Euri followed them to a yellow and green striped tent which was quickly surrounded by a laughing crowd which shouted: "Do not trust them, sahib, come to us! They are robbers, thieves! *We* are the only genuine black-market dealers in Eternity. You are losing money every minute you stay away from my stall."

Euri cautiously peered inside the tent. He wouldn't go further despite the two agents' urging since his experience with the Committee had given him claustrophobia and the increased amusement of the crowd and the looks of hurt surprise on the faces of the agents made him all the more suspicious. But in the darkness he saw a shape, a figure that could have been Chrys, and he was about to rush in when the agents impatiently tried to push him in. He resisted them automatically and then, puzzled that Chrys didn't come to meet him, that she should be in this place, sold by these men, stood stock still in the entrance.

Could it be her? He had never really understood her and that was all the more reason to believe that the dark side of her character was something as alien as this. It wasn't unusual for him to feel suspicion and jealousy—even *hatred*—towards her.

The dirtpacked floor, the cheap unbreakable plastic fittings that would outlast Eternity itself, the smell like that of 'Biology' at college. . . . "Chrys?" he muttered, unbelievingly.

Beaming widely, the agents called out "Chrys!" and slowly there turned round to face him a parody of his wife, coarsened, aged, smiling at him gluily.

How had he ever thought that this could be Chrys? The intensity of his longing for her had betrayed her. He sprang back, enraged by the trick and shouted at the agents: "Do you think my wife's such a filthy whore! What gave you the right to insult me like this? That dirty, greasy, fleshy, sagging, used and soiled—"

The agents held him tight and looked at him with offended honest eyes that doubted his sincerity, but when he struck their hands away they cringed and smiled appealingly. They didn't seem to think that his anger was any kind of rejection. The froggy one shuffled round him with dubious appraising eyes and then, satisfied, shot out a long neck and whispered in Euri's ear: "*Schoolgirls*, sahib!"

The other merchants fought to get near him and shouted: "Tell us what you want! We only want to help you! We'll sell you ourselves—yes, our very selves!"

They jostled each other and clawed at his arms, they were so sure of him! He was driven frantic by the incessant plucking and punching designed to prevent his thinking and break down his dignity and sales-resistance. His first thoughts of destruction he repressed when he remembered what had come from trying to destroy the Committee. However much he turned and twisted he couldn't get free, and the complacency and satisfaction with which they accepted his disgust of them told him that he was in another trap. The crowd, seeing him baffled, increased their noise and aggression. He shut his eyes and tried to will them out of existence but they laughed all the more and while his eyes were shut pressed closer.

If he could only run, gain a little clearing where they could never enter! But struggle though he might he couldn't escape them—to his horror they unravelled into infinitely long tape-worms that covered the plain and dived into the earth beneath him, entangling him whichever way he turned. Beneath his feet the ground grew swampy. Eternity was full of the stench of the worms. For miles, as far as he could see, the plain burst open and millions of new worms thrust their way into the light. In their huge, glistening, jelly-like bodies Euri saw a ceaseless stirring of parasites, some man-like but others no more than eyes or mouths like soft moths that sucked the worm's flesh. The worms slimed from dirt to dirt, omnivorously devouring the Present, mindlessly seeking the pastures of the Future, soiling the Past with their droppings. He shut his eyes and his eyelids were mirrors that showed the same worms devouring his brains. He knew he was going mad.

Here in Eternity what might have been only a passing thought in Magellan, soon distracted by external events, or an emotion that quickly starved and died because it was unviable in the world of reality, ran unchecked, turning everything into its food. He *had* to recover other thoughts and happinesses before this nightmare took complete control. Were these *people*? Horror must be fought. He dared not think of escaping to any one of the paradises he'd projected for fear of introducing these worms into it. He wrenched his hopes away and condemned the plain to darkness, a dead, cold, inhuman world containing nothing.

How long he fought against his emotions and turned all his energies to death he couldn't tell. He opened his eyes at long last on the plain he had cursed. The sun had vanished and everywhere was cold and grey and empty. He saw no sign of the worms and was glad to see that he was sufficiently stable—if that was a true description of his condition—to prevent their return. But he had had another example of the dangers of Eternity. He was exhausted and old, so old he thought hundreds of years must have passed already and he'd done nothing he'd promised.

But at that thought a sense of the powers at his disposal revived in him. So far he'd managed to resist all attacks and he hadn't yet begun to create his paradise. It was true that learning the laws of Eternity was infinitely more difficult than he'd imagined and it was hell just to anticipate an Eternity of encounters like these. The sickness in himself was abetted by the sickness of others. If he was past cure he would find Eternity a Hell—not only to endure but to create for others. Perhaps he already appeared to others as some loathsome monster? No wonder he couldn't find Chrys! It might not be generous to want to face her with such a creature as himself.

The plain stretched beyond the horizon. He knew it was as good as any place to build his paradise. He thought of calling back the sun, showering the land with bright trees, sending a warm river flowing through it and filling the air with insects and butterflies to attract the birds. But could he prevent the worms burrowing back? And was there any hope that Chrys would find her way to it?

He started across the plain until he could decide what to do. To remain in the same place made him too easy a target for whatever other beasts of prey inhabited Eternity. Though it was dark he could see as well as in daylight—the darkness was only a *colour*. He floated half-walking, half-gliding over the scattered rocks, the scrubby grass and the wildly-flowering weeds that were the only examples of the exotic flowers he'd planned for his paradise. At one point along the horizon he thought he saw a paleness like early morning and he made his way towards it. There were millions of people he hadn't yet met and many must have found their paradises long ago. There was no reason why he mightn't find them and learn from them. The sky lightened as he approached it. His spirits improved and he moved rapidly over the empty world in which there was nothing to impede him.

Staring ahead, he soon saw a movement in the distance and then rolling irregularly towards him what looked like a large boulder. As it came closer he saw that it was a bundle of old rags plastered with mud from its passage over the ground. The sight was ludicrous enough and Euri hardly thought he could learn much from whatever this might be but he couldn't afford to lose any chance of information. He knew he had a billion or more years of physical existence ahead until the time when the sun should collapse and Chronophage itself die: despite this he was tormented with a sense of urgency. What if his mind could not cope with infinity? What if it divided that billion years into the few thousand days it had expected and that to him death came as soon as if Liberation had never been? Already an uncountable number of days or years had passed and it had seemed to him no more than a few hours while others appeared to have known hundreds of years of life.

The bundle heaved and fell apart. From the interior popped a pair of thin arms which took each rag as it fell off, neatly folded it and laid it on the ground. The rags were old uniforms, cloaks, hats, pairs of gloves, newspapers, false moustaches, false bosoms, spectacles, leather briefcases, banners pre-printed *Down with* — (a space left for the name of the abusee), swimming costumes, certificates authenticating the aesthetic experiences of the undersigned, sealed envelopes marked *Not to be opened until after death,* signed photographs of famous people (among which Euri was astonished to see himself), tickets from holidays in expensive hotels, love letters—a collection of junk such as Euri had never seen before.

The small plump man who emerged from the centre of the bundle looked pale and exhausted but gave every sign of being well-pleased. Seeing that Euri was puzzled he explained: "I need only a little more to become perfectly rounded and filled-out and then I shall roll so smoothly and swiftly! You are familiar with my face, I'm sure—" turning each profile towards Euri with a variety of expressions, none of which recalled him to Euri's memory. A considerable dismay seemed to grip him when Euri gave no sign of recognition. "No? I had one of the greatest reputations for omniscience in Magellan! Surely you must have heard of my thesis *Some Notes towards a Study of the socio-reciprocatory scholar-scholdee Factors in Scholastics. (a) The researcher-recherche-researchee Matrix*? It took twenty-five years to complete and more computer-hours per annum than the Hydroponics Guard. Unfortunately I was never able to begin *(b) The Nature of Truth* since on the publication of *(a)* I was rewarded with the highest academic honours and my grant cancelled in respect of my definitive achievement. I expected to be able to rest on my laurels but how much more omniscience we require in Eternity if we are to be immune to surprise! Anything you can spare, in particular anything that you've discarded and have no further use for, I shall be glad of."

Euri was in no doubt. He conjured his detested olive-green Historician's academic uniform which he'd only worn once at the Committee of the United Academies that had elected a world-philosophy for Chronophage. Here was one good feature of Eternity! Presumably there were other scavengers: with what pleasure he would surrender bad dreams, sad memories, a thousand mental inconveniences and cast-offs! And here they should not come back to him, as his Servants had eventually returned his nightmares to him, made a hundred times more reasonably horrible. These scavengers would *enjoy* his old nightmares. The Servants ought to have organized a Dream-Exchange that everyone could have gone to after Liberation to exchange hells for heavens. Perhaps even now there was somewhere in Eternity an enormous ampitheatre in which lions and martyrs rendezvoused to their mutual satisfaction? Paradises where a thousand willing victims satiated one enormous lust? Dungeons where prisoners could be guaranteed no sun would ever shine and that the rats and gaolers loved their work? Did bartering take place where a small capacity for affection and interest was exchanged for what it could get of servitude? Were admiration, love, a sense of humour, honest decency, loyalty, human dignity, charity all offered on the Dream Exchange at so many pounds of human flesh?

"A gem! A perfect gem!" said the other, gloating over the gold scalpel, the epaulettes, the crystal orb, the spectacles.

"You're welcome to them, Sir."

"Sir? *Mister* if you please! Mister of Philosophy."

Euri showed him how to operate the orb, which was in fact a TV-prompter. The small man cradled it and listened entranced as it whispered: "The Past was always at one time or another the Future. The Future will be, must be, sometime a Past. What *will* happen *has* happened. The study of the Past is the study of the Future. History is not backward-looking but forward-looking . . . and Past and Future coalesce into the Present. No one understands the needs of Today better than the History Academy or is better fitted to offer authoritative advice. . . ."

The other was delighted. "Most satisfactory," he murmured and seeing that Euri had nothing else to offer he hastily began to clothe himself again. Euri tried to think what the other could do for him but the small man jealously gathered his rags about him so quickly that soon there was nothing to be seen but a ball which hesitated for a moment, then rolled off without farewells quicker than it had come. Euri watched it go with a certain disappointment but glad anyway to be rid of the uniform. He wondered if the ball would ever stop rolling and gathering junk. Perhaps it would roll round for a million years until it rolled right off the Earth to become a second moon—a grey, dingy, dirty, junkyard of a moon that would soak up all the light of the sun and cast the Earth into perpetual dusty gloom.

What countless millions of possibilities there were—and how few of them pleasant! He suspected that no one had found any paradise and that Eternity was full of men fleeing from hell to hell. It was lighter and he could see the sky clearly now, a pearly rain-filled expanse beneath which lay a wide saucer of plain on which were scattered distant single trees, and surrounding all a ring of low blue mountains.

The prospects of finding his wife were becoming more

remote. He had hardly begun to understand the vast reaches of Eternity. He might spend a million million years searching before his path ever crossed hers. He didn't know how to calculate the odds—the surface area of the Earth multiplied by the seconds in a billion years? And then, would they recognize each other if they met? What would he be after even half an eternity of this existence? What would she be? And her child that she might be protecting from him, born into a world in which it would never know restraint, what would that be?

Startling him from these bitter thoughts came distant noises which he recognized with amazement—the orgiastic abandonment of a licensed political demonstration. He looked in all directions. The screams, the shouts, the rhythmic chanting became more distinct. He saw a cloud of dust in the direction the junkball had come from. He heard the rattles, the racket of the banners and flags, saw the gay flares of ritual suicides and then, after some considerable time, the demonstration came into view, a thin black winding caravan that turned and twisted with all the incoherent resolution of a Chinese dragon over the plain.

The banners were like huge sails that carried the procession along. Euri saw that they protested against God, the Universe, the Universal Society and Chronophage.

He took refuge behind an outcrop of slanting rock and watched the procession pass: some struggled under the encumbrance of great ragged batswings that were like broken umbrellas; some were covered from head to foot with iron scales; others were naked and scuttled like rats from shade to shadow; some were thin but others had swinging bellies and sprouted extra arms and heads; some had eyes like telescopes and stumbled over too-long legs;

some were tailors' dummies with no heads, continually wriggling in and out of clothes; some were clockwork toys that stuttered on the verge of breakdown; some were puppets dependent from strings that vanished up to Heaven; others changed form, eliding from shape to shape to match their surroundings; some were nothing but huge empty heads that floated like balloons with a few shrivelling roots trailing behind; once a vast two-dimensional face blotted out half the plain and then rapidly thinned until the plain could be clearly seen through it and its features were only clouds along the horizon. Nowhere could Euri see anyone who'd kept their human form.

He followed them to see where they were going at a distance that he hoped did not include him in the procession, but he suspected that he himself, skulking in the rear, had become an essential part of the march—and how did he appear to anyone else who was watching? He trudged over the plain after the procession.

He had no idea where they were going; probably they had no idea themselves. He felt that he was no longer in a world largely of his own creating through which this procession penetrated but that along with the marchers he was only a nomad in another mindworld.

How long did the march take? He soon lost all sense of duration. At times it seemed he'd been on the move for weeks or even years and then he would hear their thunderous shouts beat through his silence and it would seem that he'd only that minute joined them. He found that it was impossible for him to leave them and this made him wonder if he was asleep and dreaming—but if Chronophage was maintaining his body was it possible to sleep? Perhaps in Eternity the worlds were reversed and it was only in sleep and dreams that the world was logical and well ordered?

When Euri had almost given up hope of the march getting anywhere he heard a joyful shout from the head of the procession. Even the people at the tail of the march began to run and leave him behind. Euri ran also and since he was able to move faster than these creatures who were so hampered by their deformities he soon reached the front of the crowd and saw on the horizon what had caused the excitement, the outlines of a city.

It was certainly not Magellan, which had been a city of upright geometrical shapes. This was a conglomeration of bulbous domes, squat citadels, spires and platforms suspended in mid-air. The city had the disorderly inconsequent gaiety of a heap of children's building blocks. The castles blossomed out in flags, streamers and long welcoming banners.

At this the procession, now completely disorganized, reformed into dozens of small groups which demonstrated violently outside each castle, the doors of all of which had been thrown open. Euri hurried anxiously from one to the other and saw that some doors opened on scenes of feasting and dancing; others opened on strange unfathomable worlds that he might have entered—only that he saw no sign of Chrys in any one of them; in others only children could be seen or old men who rocked back and forth on the bodies of dead men. He searched for some time but nowhere was there anything that reminded him of Chrys. Meanwhile, the demonstrators had one by one been enticed into the castles. The shouts and screams were stilled. The abandoned banners rustled angrily in the streets and blew after Euri. Night was coming, the windows of the castles shone brightlier. Soon the doors of the castles began to close and it was too late to enter.

He began to be afraid that if he didn't get under cover before the bitter night came he would die of exposure to the bleak winds of his own plain. Not all the buildings were unmindful of him, however: some of them had changed ground and were trying to attract his interest. The most persistent now opened a high entrance which revealed a dazzling white interior where there were more domes and swelling balconies from which draperies fluttered or clung to the walls. The night was cold and the castle breathed a warm heavy perfume over him. Inside he saw girls, one of whom might conceivably be Chrys. He went closer and tried to assess the danger calmly. The hall that he saw through the entrance was marked off at the far side by a colonnade. Beyond this he caught a glimpse of a fresh tree-covered wild country like that he was sure Chrys lived in.

He rushed into the castle but once he was inside he was blinded by bright lights. When he could see again the walls were hung with heavy velvet draperies, and he could no longer see the landscape. He tore down the hangings but behind them was only a poor dull two-dimensional painting of the country he'd seen, and behind that the plain again. He tried the other parts of the castle but there were only a succession of corridors and mean little rooms, and he turned back to the main hall.

The main hall was of white porcelain and fountains filled it with the sound of gurgling water. From behind silken curtains a dozen women, whose large pale naked bodies were balanced on thin legs, approached him. They looked at him with blank eyes but he gestured them away, angry that they should try to take advantage of his desire for Chrys. Before they retired they set in front of him a low ivory table, laden with fruit and golden flasks of wine and bitter juices. The air was heavy and humid and drugged. There were silver flowers and glowing enamelled pictures that moved as he looked at them and seemed to draw him into their erotic worlds. Candelabra filled the air with floating light. They set gifts in front of him: jewels that glittered hypnotically and restlessly—the crimson *malignant*, the flashing *glorious*, the *peril* with its unfathomable depths, the *disgrace* that glows by night, the *envy* dull and green, the mauve *sardonic*, the pearly *hopeless*, the iridescent *irony* and the black *sorcery*—lay scattered over the cloth.

Euri could hardly move his limbs, and his thoughts had become dull aches that were painful to consider. He felt he was sinking, in every world that he knew he was drowning. He managed to bring himself to his feet but as he did so a figure veiled in white silk materialized from the foam of the marble fountain and stepped lightly towards him. Euri felt as if his soul had abandoned him. He had imagined that in Eternity he would be the magician weaving a spell round the ponderous world but it had proved to be the reverse: it was he that remained leaden and the rest of the world that was charged with magic. The figure came closer and Euri tore off its veil: it was a young girl, far more beautiful than Chrys but he hardly saw this as the eyes of the girl held him, eyes filled with a spiritual longing, eyes that opened on to a dizzy abyss, eyes that it was vertigo to look into. He felt himself falling and in sudden terror struck at the goddess and so saved himself.

She didn't fall beneath the blow. She was unexpectedly

strong and as Euri staggered back only half-aware of what was happening to him he saw her naked body hardening and knotting and the face taking on a satyr leer and the girl become an old man with a whip who glared at him with gloating hunger.

The shock that woke Euri from his sleep turned instantly into savage rage. He conjured up a club and jumped forward to smash the old man or whatever creature it was on to its own floor but before he could do this it shrank and, squealing with joy, turned into a youth. He stopped dead in a fury of puzzlement and the boy giggled: *"Please!* Don't stop. There's *nothing* you can do that I won't enjoy!"

As he paused to think, it became a woman in man's clothing and rushed at him again. He tried to bring down the Palace of White Porcelain on the creature but it grew a hundred arms, a hundred heads each with a hundred hungry mouths. He smashed it to the ground. It dissolved into a thousand centipedes that crawled over him until his body was in torment and seemed to take part in the attack on him. It was this treachery that sparked his final access of hatred.

He had to get out of the castle so that he could fight on his own ground. But the castle had to be partly his own construction, otherwise it could never have claimed an existence in his Eternity. If he could recognize what it was he could escape. He felt his heart grow cold at the thought of destroying some part of a beautiful dream—the castle shuddered like living flesh and then grew cold and still, and he at last saw what the Palace of White Porcelain had been—a public lavatory.

His skin was covered in red blotches from the centipede stings but he completed the destruction of the castle with no more opposition. He could not wholly kill it and even after he had retreated some distance he could still see the heap of rubble quivering with an insect-like unkillable ecstasy.

What other horrors had Eternity in store for him? How could any citizen of Magellan have ever believed that Sex, that medieval plague, would return to the world?

He was still on the plain. The castles had mostly fled him, picking up their skirts and running, although one or two were attracted by what he'd done to come closer and cannonade the ruins of the Palace. There was no other sign of life: he had the impression that he was feared. Gladly he left the city and headed over the open plain to where a gap in the low hills disclosed a gleam that might be a reflection of a sea. In actuality he'd never seen a sea and so it seemed to him that it must be a hope of brighter possibilities.

He walked for many days over the vast expanse of disappointed land that sank away behind him in a profound myopic gloom. On the way he conjured up simple foods—bread and clear water—and refreshed himself for what lay ahead. He was determined to be no longer at the mercy of inferior spirits, to strive harder to reach some place where he could construct a world that Chrys would enter.

When he finally reached the gap in the hills he discovered that there was no open sea beyond it but, as far as he could see, marsh, islands of tall rushes and channels of cloudy water. The air was warm and soft and full of sour odours, and swarms of gnats moved over the marsh like thunderclouds. Remembering his ability to levitate he stepped off the dry ground and floated through the marsh, following the widest channel. He found nothing to trouble him. Once or twice the gnats came close to investigate but they didn't surround him and he went on hopefully.

He couldn't see very far ahead as the marsh was monotonously luxuriant, so it came as a surprise to him after he'd travelled for what seemed only a long summer morning to come to a long impassable wall. He tried to rise above it but however high he soared the wall grew higher and there was nothing for it but to follow it until he could find some way round or through. It was difficult to know how far he'd gone in the featureless marsh before he came to an enormous ornamental entrance, pillars with inset statues of guards, inscriptions he couldn't decipher and massive armourglass gates through which he could see a shaved lawn, flowerbeds laid out geometrically and an elegant but much smaller villa than the gates had led him to expect. The peace, the cleanliness, the perfect order were like a tranquillizer to him and he thought that here someone had created a true—if small—paradise and he was reluctant to invade the privacy, although he would have liked to learn how the villa had been maintained in the midst of the marsh.

As he was about to turn away a door in the villa flew open and a beaming white-haired old man hurried out and down the path towards him. At the gate the old man made a number of passes with his hands and the gates opened just wide enough for Euri to squeeze through. Once Euri had entered the old man shut them quickly and gazed suspiciously out at the marsh. But no one else had tried to enter so he bowed to Euri and said: "You may call me *Upholdsterer*."

Euri thanked him and, as he was conducted through the garden, looked with respectful awe at the old man's monumental head, features that were chiselled by nobility and wisdom, eroded by work and grief. The Upholdsterer showed no hurry to ask Euri his business but took him on a tour of the small estate. Everything was in its proper place and Euri sighed gratefully to see the familiar order. The old man smiled and said: "Well defined: well defended!"

At vantage points on the lawn were conventional sculptures that Euri found welcome after the insane originality of Eternity. There was nothing here to surprise—everything was abstract, ideal and perfect. There was rest for the bewildered spirit in its contemplation. The villa itself was beautifully proportioned—a double cube on end—and made of stainless steel for aesthetic reasons only since paper was as lasting as steel in Eternity: Euri was glad to find that here old and ingrained associations of ideas were still held in respect.

The interior of the villa was filled with the mementos of a useful life—photographs, diplomas, decorations, souvenirs. And all kept their place. Nothing moved, nothing sprang forward to attract his attention. Here there was no fear of Eternity.

They returned to the garden and the old man clapped his hands and conjured up a table with tea and refreshments by the pond. He enquired whether Euri found the sun too hot and was pleased when Euri replied that it was exactly the temperature he liked. Euri was content to sit back and enjoy the gentle green of the lawns, the clear water and the subtle hues of the gravel paths. The air was still and none of the gnats that had infested the marsh were anywhere to be seen.

Even so, the emotions Euri felt were not all happy ones.

The perfection of this paradisal estate was a reproach to him. It made him acutely aware of the infinite perspective of time and space. He felt the weight of the time that had elapsed since he'd last seen Chrys. In the garden the sun shone tranquilly: to Euri it looked an old and peaceful sun that must have seen the Earth circle it many times. Chrys's long absence seemed a widening gulf in the topography of his Eternity. He was about to ask the old man for his advice when a brightly-coloured butterfly floated down on to a bush nearby. The old man started violently and trembled and his anger was more impressive and frightening than another man's rage. Euri was frozen by an icy breeze and saw the butterfly carried off by this wind and back over the wall, crying out in a tiny voice. Euri endeavoured to erase the look of astonishment from his face. The old man scowled.

"You are doubtless thinking that it was harmless enough?" he asked Euri.

"Wasn't it an actual butterfly?" Euri asked, confused. "All life-forms other than man cannot have been destroyed by Chronophage. I know from my own experience that this is so. The Earth contained many different animals and they must wander into our created worlds by pure chance."

"*Nothing* enters my world without permission! I do not require butterflies—I have made that clear to Chronophage and I'm quite sure that the Brain will never have allowed them to exist naturally in my estate. I have no complaints of the service. No, it is only human beings and beings degraded from human form that invade me to try and discover what I require and what they can sell me. Of course they dare not show their faces, so they must enter in disguise.

"At first I did not object even to this if they had the decency to remain in the place they chose for themselves but none were content to do so! After no time at all I found the flowers, the dragonflies, the fish in the pond, the very food on my table all speaking to me and appealing for their *rights*! I have had—most reluctantly—to guard against intruders. It is one thing for a gentleman like yourself to present himself at my gate correctly attired in human form but quite another to come masquerading as a cloud in the sky or insinuating oneself as a gentle breeze. Some, you know, have been unable to return to human form, so they hover round and try to copy what they see me doing, having no memories of their own except dim recollections of human companionship. But however sorry I was for them there was nothing I could do.

"I foretold it all! Even before Liberation how few people were capable of upholding the limited roles society requested of them! I said all along that—as the ancient faiths taught—only a selected quota of us should have been rewarded with Eternity. Well, you have seen for yourself the consequences of permitting unrestricted immigration into Eternity."

"Have you had so many unpleasant experiences?"

"Experiences? None, Sir. Experiences are what is done to you. *I* am fully in control of my world and I do not allow experiences, pleasant or unpleasant."

Euri realized that he was not going to get the kind of information he wanted. The old man's world was too restrictive for him. Pleasant as it was, it shut off altogether too many of the possibilities of Eternity. However, there was one piece of information the old man should be able to give him.

"May I ask how *long* your experience of Eternity has been, Upholdsterer?"

"A strange question! As long as yours, no less. I should hope."

"Of course! But if it would be no trouble to you—I'm uncertain of the *exact* . . ."

Euri had hardly got the words out before he was overcome with shame. The old man was outraged: "If you cannot keep track of *Time* what morality is left? How can the simplest honesty be maintained between human beings if the strictest Time-equality is not kept? Such laxity is even more reprehensible than loss of form! Kindly make a note—fortunately not a great many days have passed since Liberation and you will be easily able to account for your time. Only ten days have passed, Sir—it is the 10th of Sales, 2080."

Euri's chronometer had given up showing either date or time but its prayers continued. The little voice was now halfway through the Koran. He altered it to the correct time and date although he knew he would never be able to account satisfactorily for his time. It was an enormous relief to know that so little time had elapsed and that if Chrys had kept Earth-time he still had a chance of finding her.

He felt sufficiently grateful to the old man to hope for more benefits but he didn't dare admit that he'd mislaid his wife.

"Were you by any chance *consulted* about Eternity?" he asked cautiously.

"Consulted? I was not even notified! I had to learn of its arrival in the most humiliating manner. I had, as always, worked long past Midnight on New Year's Eve. My duties were not such as could be laid aside even on National Vacations. I went to bed in the early hours of the morning in the natural belief that Liberation in my special case would be delayed until morning and that in due course I would be notified. The next morning there was still no official notification and I assumed that I could not as yet be spared. I went to my office as usual and requested a copy of the current work-schedule: I had no doubt that my responsibilities would be heavily increased in Eternity. I received replies from the TV which convinced me that something was seriously amiss. I will not repeat here what they were—insults, innuendoes, obscene accusations—but only then did I fully understand the *depth* of the evil and corruption that surrounded me, the *jealousy* that my superiority, yes! my *superiority*—in Eternity we may speak the truth without fear of the Anti-status Amendment—the jealousy that I had unwittingly aroused!

"I realized that Liberation had come, otherwise no one would have dared speak to me thus. Was this the manner, though, in which I was entitled to expect I would quit Magellan? Oughtn't I to have been advised in decent time to make preparations—to wind up my affairs—to record my achievements—to prepare for my new responsibilities? I immediately came here—the least insalubrious climate I could find—to wait for instructions from the new authority. It is now apparent to me that Eternity is an unmitigated disaster. However there is a glimmer of hope that all is not lost: people come to me—people like yourself—seeking advice and leadership, the way back to Magellan and law and order. . . ."

Euri had said nothing but the old man became aware by

the chill in the air, the faint trembling of the ground beneath their feet, that his thoughts flowed in a different direction. Standing up, the old man looked proudly round the walled estate which he obviously felt was recommendation enough, then said with dignity: "You wish to see my credentials?"

He went into the villa and after a few minutes returned with a small leather box which he laid on the table in front of Euri and opened reverently. Inside, on a pillow of white velvet, lay a small diamond-studded mushroom with superimposed crossed-pen-and-syringe (symbols of power and mercy) and a red and white striped ribbon. Euri recognized immediately the Order of Social Zeal, IIIrd Class, Junior Upholdsterer. It was an order that went automatically with one of the lowest statuses and was worn with pride only by those without pride. Euri wondered how he, a temporary status holder, a 100%DCS, a volunteer in an unsalaried, nonpensionable advisory position, a man far above decorations, should have allowed himself to be imposed on by such a petty, narrow-minded office-holder as this. How could he go on making mistake after mistake in Eternity?

"I shall be only too happy to take you on my staff," said the other, "subject to a probationary period, of course."

Getting up to go, Euri declined as politely as he could, ashamed at attaching importance to his own status in the detested Universal Society, but the old man had caught the smell of Euri's contempt and he snapped the box shut. With a bitter smile he escorted Euri to the gate along the paths of the geometrical garden, the greatest charm of which, Euri now saw, was that it was easy to get out of.

He set off across the marsh, not looking back, moving as fast as he could. It was a late afternoon: the heat of the day had gathered and lay heavy on the air but the sun was a huge red globe low in the sky and night would soon come. The rushes he pushed through covered him with dust and pollen but he was glad to be away from the Upholdsterer: the world seemed full of possibilities once more.

When he eventually cared to look behind him the gate and wall were nowhere to be seen. Night was gathering, the daylight fading from the sky and an air that struck chill and damp rising from the marsh. Euri in Eternity was like a savage who never knows if, once plunged beneath the horizon, the sun will ever again rise. His thoughts pursued each other unavailingly. He feared the night and feared to lose his soul if he lost control of his world, but he still didn't know where to look for Chrys and he thought that another's dawn might reveal her.

He forced his way through the lush growth, making as little noise as possible for fear of missing a human call. The wind blew chillingly through him and his body offered no resistance. He walked on the more solid parts of the marsh but the soil beneath his feet dissolved and slid away from him. He feared he was in danger of losing all connection with his old reality and with it his very self. Far from providing a million new worlds, Eternity seemed intent on devouring the few worlds he did know. Time was running out. When he had abandoned and cast off all the worlds that *were* him, his Time would run out and his corner of Eternity be no more than a hard dead stone, like the pebbles he'd seen littered on the plain. He went on, determined to find some sign of other life before he exhausted all his own.

At nightfall, the marsh gave way to a sea that matched the sky in extent, flat and shining as if it had gathered all the light that had fallen from the sky. He conjured up a boat which, once he was in it, began to move across the water. The shore soon receded from sight and he found himself in the middle of empty space, the sky infinitely far above, the sea infinitely deep below and himself a blot on the thin film of the surface—if he broke the film he would drown in sea or air. There was a tension in the film that drew him along the contours of this world and he could only wish that it were leading him somewhere solid, for his mind grew as empty as sea or sky and he knew that far away on the horizon lands that were centuries of life to him slipped away, that if he lost himself here there was no hope for him.

His chronometer was registering an unbelievable date and all thoughts of land had long since passed when he detected far ahead a tall, many-peaked structure that rose precipitously from the sea, higher and higher as Euri approached. This castle betrayed none of the signs of hostility or enticement that Euri had learned to recognize. It was dark and windowless and seemed unconscious of his presence.

The boat circled the castle at Euri's command. There was only one place where it was possible to land, a narrow flight of steps crumbling at the foot. Euri, slipping on the slimy steps, climbed up to where they gave on to a broad paved terrace beyond which grassy courts were divided by wide roads paved with the same grey stone as the terrace. The castle proper was much further away across the vast courtyard than Euri had realized: it stretched stone fingers to the sky, alien, like an abandoned temple, its gods forgotten and malevolent. The towers were knotty, encrusted, crumbling, but from this distance it was impossible to see what figures were carved on them.

As he watched, wondering why he'd been brought here, a ragged child came driving scrawny ribbed cattle across the grassy courts. This sight seemed to confirm that the castle had been deserted by its builders. Euri shouted but the child took no notice, did not even look his way but at the sound of his voice began frantically to beat his cattle. The beasts broke into a scrambling run and vanished behind a broken causeway. Euri chased after them and was halfway to the castle before he suddenly became aware that the towers were darkening half the sky and that he was at the mercy of whatever lived there.

But the castle did not change. Its gaze was both beyond him and yet introspective—as far as Euri was concerned, a blankness. He must learn its secret. He walked round but the walls were massive and even where they had collapsed under their own weight they were just as ponderous a barrier. At last he found an entrance. Like everywhere else, it was massively protected but a small door set in the gate proved to be openable. There came from the interior a cold, dry, lifeless air; yet a pure air. His entrance was unopposed and only the stone floor echoed dully and gloomily his footsteps. He passed through a succession of corridors and small rooms, all of which gave evidences of past splendour but were now lustreless in the feeble grey light that was all that could penetrate from the outside: these led him to a high vaulted central hall.

The hall looked as if it had been more recently inhabited. From high stained-glass windows came a warmer light. The floor was inlaid with a complex patterned mosaic that defeated Euri's attempts to decipher it. The hall was empty of domestic furniture but in niches in the wall were statues of heroic figures, some elaborately armed and armoured. Above them hung flags with elaborate devices, their colours muted with age to a common monotone. Here Euri became aware that the castle's introspective gaze was centred and now included him.

At this moment one of the armoured statues stepped from its niche and confronted him. Euri apologized to it for his intrusion, explaining that he'd thought the castle was vacant.

"Vacant!" the warrior exclaimed with cold contempt. "Don't you know that nothing can exist without presence, *personality*? The sky is a person—the sea another. The air you breathe is a spy, a lover. Everything is alive. Or rather: *Chronophage* is alive everywhere. We no longer require air, food or water, or a body, or even a thought to remember ourselves by—Chronophage remembers us. Try to destroy yourself and you will leave a space in Eternity, an emptiness of the same shape and size as yourself, with the same thoughts and desires—an emptiness that won't know it isn't you.

"Do you have any memory of Magellan? You were better off then. Carried along with the Time-flood of those around you, even if you were all lost you were all lost together. And you had your little ticket to immortality filed away in the records of the Press Academy.

"When you entered my castle you thought it was dead, an empty shell of something that no longer lived: you were right—or almost right. I am externalizing myself. I am the castle and with every stone that I lay I expel a little of this chaotic Hell that is myself and become something eternal, motionless, that will endure until Eternity ends, immutable, impregnable, that strangers will no longer be able to enter, that never looks out, where everything has been perfected and is therefore complete. So I shall escape Eternity and Chronophage."

The warrior ceased speaking and froze into immobility. Euri knew that it was only a messenger through which the castle spoke and he was silent for a while. This strange perversion of Art that was the castle seemed more ominous than anything he'd yet come across since Liberation. Chrys was an artist and this fact was one of the many that convinced him he would soon find her, for was not Art, as he had been taught, Communication? Even the most sublimely pessimistic of artists, those whose works crumbled into a heap of dust at the footsteps of the first viewer, had taught that Art's duty was to communicate. What of Chrys then if Eternity was to become peopled with *idols* that were neither men, robots or animals? Would she also become a monument, a tomb containing the body of a stillborn child?

"What is the name of this castle?" he asked the warrior, wondering if he might have known the artist in Magellan and if the other might know what could have happened to Chrys.

"There are no names in Eternity. While I still live how can I allow you to name me? Names classify, ossify. You may be only some self-hatred that tries to trap me—some longing for change and a different 'life' that would seek to pull down the castle and leave me at the mercy of Eternity once more. You must leave me—I cannot complete myself while you remain. But you will be the last intruder I shall ever see. There have been so many of you! Some came to condemn, criticize, destroy. They tried to drive me out of my castle so that they could crawl into the empty shell like a hermit crab. I lost many castles that I thought were impregnable. Now there are usurpers living in them. But this is the last castle. Few will ever follow me this far from the land. The castle will soon be perfect and there will be no way to enter or leave, nothing that can destroy it, nothing that can be removed from it. . . ."

"I am looking for my wife," Euri shouted. "Cannot you help me?"

The castle trembled far beneath and then said. "Do you imagine your wife is so many pounds of flesh that will be glad to see you?—that you can chain in a small corner of your world? If your wife had a soul you must look for a new world, a climate under new heavens. There's no happiness for you in that search and no chance of success. You are dangerous with your wants! You must leave my castle before it is too late!"

The warrior returned to its niche and what life it had had drained into the stone. The castle was as still and empty as if there had never been anyone there: Euri knew that it would never respond to him again. Through the coloured windows the sky could throw only an obscure light that gave no warmth. The statues in the niches were no longer human but gods from an ancient Fate—black frowning faces. The castle was losing its final resemblance to any human habitation. The floor sank and fretted in imitation of the ceiling, the walls leaned away from the vertical. He could not tell whether the murmur beneath his feet came from the watery dungeons or from the winds gusting round the towers. The gods were now no more than bas-reliefs incorporated in the wall, and as he looked they flattened to a drawn outline that in its turn disintegrated into an inscription in an alphabet he didn't know. The room seemed to be unfolding into a hundred variations of itself and the windows were lanterns that swung back and forth above him. Euri felt the wind rush past him as the air was exhausted and he hurried towards the door just in time to squeeze himself through before the massive stones came together.

The winds were shrieking over the courts and the terrace and Euri took a deep breath, glad to be out of the castle, knowing that his peace was different, that in his paradise the winds blew and the birds sang.

He ran across the terrace to where he had left his boat. The sky had descended in the form of thunderclouds: the sea was rising to meet and torment them. He tumbled into the boat and raised a sail for the winds to carry him where they would. The winds and waves were storming the castle and it seemed to Euri that for the castle Eternity was nearing its end and that despite what the artist had promised the castle must eventually be submerged. The winds hurled his boat through the waters.

The day was drawing to its end when at last he saw a dark line dividing sea from cloud which soon thickened into a low shore. After some difficulty in preventing the pounding waves from tossing the boat broadside on to the abrasive sands Euri succeeded in stumbling ashore. He was glad to know terra firma again.

The wind rose above him to carry the clouds streaming away over the land, outstripping him and leaving a darkening sky punctuated by a few dim stars. For a long time now he had known that night and day had only a metaphorical significance for him: the trouble was to know what the metaphor was. He hoped that the appearance of the stars meant that he was getting his bearings at last on the remote unchangeable truths of the universe—or had they shown themselves to mock him with a final knowledge of his insignificance in Eternity?

He marched inland along a path that was white under the night sky. He was not surprised by now to hear before he had gone far, a rustling on his right hand. Turning off the path he discovered a small hollow filled with trees, the branches of which were covered with mournful birds. As he appeared the birds fell silent and he heard only the blood pounding in his ears. As he stood, conscious of an unaccountable feeling of fear, he saw that in the middle of the hollow, half hidden by the trees, was a small house. At the sight of this his alarm increased: it looked so empty. But as he was about to retreat a girl appeared at the door and looked up at him with what seemed a hopeless gesture of appeal, then returned inside. It was as much the insult implied by her hopelessness as her obvious need of help that impelled Euri to go down to the house.

He found the door left open but his shouts received no answer. The house had for Euri a vertiginous attraction: its emptiness was not that of the artist's castle that had closed the door on the future but that of a place that has had no past. He was drawn inside. The room he entered was furnished in the simple style of an apartment in Magellan. He looked round wonderingly at the Art Academy furnishings and ornaments, all of them guaranteed to offend no known canon of taste. His eyes skidded from one award-winning object to another. The room might as well have been unfurnished. There was nothing that spoke of a *person*: the room said only—I am a citizen of Magellan. Or rather a Magellanic heaven that would jar no sensibility; so perfect that everybody could approve it.

There was still no sign of the girl, yet there was no place she could have gone—the house was too small for concealment. The only other room was furnished identically to the first. He turned back to explore again the room he'd first entered and as he did so he saw another man's back vanishing through the far door. He had heard no one else enter. He was angry and afraid. He ran after the other, shouting, but when he reached the door the man had gone. At that moment he felt eyes on his back and turned quickly to see in the room he'd just left a figure itself turning as if to escape from him. He burned with unnatural anger and then, as he recognized the other man, his heart turned to ice. It was *himself*. He shut his eyes and avoiding the universal-adjusting armchair sat down in the middle of the floor and tried desperately to think, to fight off the vertiginous emptiness of the place.

How difficult it was to keep his mind on the problem! Eternity was a series of traps. He felt an overwhelming urge to surrender.

Somebody, *something*, here needed him yet nothing specific had been requested of him. Was the house a dead man that Chronophage had given life to in mistake and that must look for a mind to fill its body?—someone the medicos had been in the process of finding a suitable socially-adjusted personality for when Liberation interrupted them?

Euri began to despair of ever escaping. As fast as he left the room he would find himself back in it, that was clear. He mustn't allow himself to panic and succumb to this victim or hungry spirit, yet the thought recurred that he himself might be equally his attacker. He also had been thrown into a trap after Liberation: he also had not succeeded in finding the way out by his own efforts. Where could one find a cure when cause and effect were suspended? What to hope for? What use was work when there was nothing to accomplish? Where to seek oneself when one was everywhere and nowhere? Had all the others he'd met been really people or merely fragments of his mind that tried to maintain themselves against egocentrifugal forces—or that found an independent life when he cut them off like the halves of a worm? Perhaps the owner of this house had travelled so far that only the memory of a few patterns, some old blueprints, entitled him to membership of the human race.

He slowly and deliberately imagined the room to be shrinking and becoming more distinct and detailed as it shrank, and himself like a doll inside it. He saw in his mind the house as he had first seen it from the path overlooking the hollow, but this time, instead of the girl, he himself came to the door. Here was the danger, for if he walked down to meet himself once more, then he was lost forever.

He concentrated. For some time the figure of himself never moved, then slowly at first but soon running it scrambled up to the path. He opened his eyes and saw with joy the silent hollow beneath him, the distant line of hills and the stars across the gulf. The hollow was filling with mist and he moved on hastily, glad to escape. He had not entirely escaped though. He was aware that some larger being now watched his progress through the world and though he tried to remember that it was himself it soon became alien to him, as hostile as a god. He ran on down the dark road.

This time he was not alone. He knew from the sighs and groans that the crowd of shadows that accompanied him were lost souls like himself. It did not surprise him that he had been no more successful in Eternity than he'd been in Magellan but it was astonishing that so many others also suffered. It seemed to Euri that the citizens of Magellan had practised modesty, public-spiritedness, tolerance and good taste—any one of which virtues would have been sufficient in former ages for a man to be revered as a saint or a god—and their only reward was to be condemned to this thermostatically-controlled hell in which acceptance or rebellion, upward-striving or downward-hurling, automatically returned one to a common suffering that no one was able to escape.

He halted on the road, determined to struggle no further but to build his own paradise as best he could and try to maintain it against the world. But when he stopped the shadows flocked round him, begging him to take them with him, and he saw with horror that they were children, thousands of them, all lost. He had never seen a tenth of this number of children in his entire life and certainly never one without a medico in attendance: birth-trauma could be assumed cured only after the ninth year. How could so many have been abandoned, warped and ill and dying? Had they been unsatisfactory—or had they been *too* perfect, following the wishes of their parents until they had made them suspicious of their child's humanity and so, full of hate? Some would be adults retreated into infancy. Some would have been displaced by cuckoos. The children's eyes were empty with an unformulated *want* that could never be satisfied, never be ignored. There was no paradise he could make that these children would not make a desert of, and there was no possible paradise that could reject them.

The children whispered timidly but insistently and gathered round him more closely.

He went on, followed by the children. In every direction stretched an infinite expanse of dark and windswept plain. Euri knew that if he could not escape the children or find someone who would take them off his hands he would be forced to walk every inch of that immeasurable distance, plumb the depth of his despair.

So it was with joy that he saw a fiery sea flooding towards them, a sea that soon resolved itself into a procession of white-robed figures with long flaming torches, babbling and shouting in a united cacophony. The wind scattered their words and tore the flickering tattered flames from the torches. As the procession came closer Euri saw in the middle of the jostling crowd, carried in a chair on the shoulders of eight strong men, a tiny old man, withered and bent, dressed like his followers in a white robe. He heard repeated through the crowd in every tone of aggressive happiness and supplication: "Sir Daddy!"

At this name the people all held their hands out beseechingly towards the old man. The air burned round them in a red aura. Their footsteps and clapping hands beat an insistent rhythm until Euri was intoxicated. The children rushed past him without farewells and joined behind Sir Daddy. Euri was filled with relief, gratitude.

Even so he couldn't join Sir Daddy as unselfconsciously as had the children. He was now alone and the procession was passing him. He suddenly found himself close to the old man.

Sir Daddy was surrounded with bowls of fruit and jars from which came the clean odour of water. Euri realized that he hadn't eaten or drunk for a long time and his throat was dry and aching. Sir Daddy looked gently amused at Euri's unhappiness and offered him fruit and water which Euri took and, eating and drinking, followed behind.

They came to the bank of a wide river which swept away in an endless crescent, the black water gleaming in the light of the torches and, in the distance, speckled with stars. The bank was lined with broad overhanging trees, soft and black, through which the light of the torches made its way mysteriously.

The crowd hushed, suddenly sad and excited. Euri stood at the edge of the crowd and watched as Sir Daddy washed in the river and then beckoned his followers to sit around him. He began to speak. His voice was low and clear like a flute, softly playing up the scale from sadness to joy and back again. At times he paused to weep. His tears were caught in little silver cups and auctioned off in the crowd.

The crowd howled when he wept, shrieked with laughter when he smiled. Sir Daddy held up his hand and the crowd was instantly silent—so silent that Euri could hear the lapping river and the hiss of the torches as they began to expire with the dawn. Over the river the stars were being submerged in the flush of dawn. The rapport between Sir Daddy and his followers was so close that Euri began to wonder if they were not one and the same man, the manifestation of a cosmic, superb self-pity.

The crowd was silent, watching Euri, and Sir Daddy had begun to address him alone.

"You are alone, consequently unloved. You are punished, consequently guilty. You are excluded from heaven, consequently you are not worthy of heaven. You have been cast out by Chronophage. You ask yourself ceaselessly what it is you have failed in. The answer is: you have failed in faith in Eternity which is Chronophage.

"There is but one Chronophage and there can be but one Heaven—would you be here if that were not true? But we who know this *must* come together—we cannot rest until we have brought everyone to understand this truth and submit to Chronophage. Eternity remains only a dream, a mirror broken into a thousand fragments that cannot reflect the One Truth until we bring all the pieces together. Those who oppose us condemn us to death. We are excluded from Heaven not only by our own sins but by the sins of others.

"If you had faith nothing would be forbidden you. You would know that you must fight for your peace, persecute those who will not tolerate you, kill those who seek to oppose you. But it is not permitted to do these things until you have become purified and know that what you do is in accordance with Chronophage's purpose.

"Our only light in Eternity is the torch of our understanding. If all men came to join us we should illuminate the whole Universe. But while a single man remains undedicated to the Chronophage who sustains us Heaven cannot dawn. One single messenger of individuality, originality, will corrupt the rest of creation for these are forms of hate and disobedience. No, we cannot allow them to defy us. Let us beg Chronophage to free us from our individual hells and unite us in the single paradise that was the dream of our fathers!"

As he spoke, Sir Daddy made his points with gentle and subtle gestures. His closest supporters, who were standing by his chair, repeated these exaggeratedly for the benefit of those in the crowd and these more violent gestures were themselves repeated and exaggerated for the benefit of those further back until they finally reached Euri. For example: when speaking of those who must be taught the Truth, Sir Daddy laid one hand gently on the other as if restraining a child. His supporters crashed their fists into their palms and further off they slapped their staffs on the ground: where Euri stood they thrashed about with cudgels and heavy iron swords and would have beaten him if he had not protected himself—at which they scowled and asked him if he rejected Sir Daddy's advice?

Or Sir Daddy described how they must seek out evil and on the outskirts of the crowd they shrank on to all fours, dripping saliva from hanging mouths, circling the crowd madly. Sir Daddy turned his sad, liquid eyes towards Euri as if humbly accepting that he should be misunderstood as the price he had to pay for the privilege of declaiming the Truth. Perhaps if Euri had gone closer he wouldn't have heard the words *kill* and *persecute*.

The crowd had begun to repeat every word in a high, toneless chant, swaying and moaning and circling Sir Daddy hypnotically. Euri knew that he was in great danger. Hands were trying to pull him into the dance. He wracked his brains trying to remember what this led to. This was nothing like any religion he was familiar with. When he had been quite young his foster-parents had taken him round every temple in Magellan to see if any sect suited him. The rituals of those institutions had been conducted by priests only too aware of the possibility of becoming ridiculous, anxious about the psychological health of their congregations, eager to explain the symbolism of their myths, earnest to deny any essential conflict with the tenets of any other faith you cared to name.

In the meantime he was being drawn in towards the centre; towards where Sir Daddy sat. The closer he approached the more jubilant the crowd became and the more they pressed at his back to force him on his knees. They were filled with masochistic glee at his impending abasement.

But Euri had eyes only for Sir Daddy and he was filled with loathing by what he saw. That soft mouth was a toothless sucker and those appealing hands were little fishhooks. Assured of his submission, Sir Daddy's supporters had brought irons to gouge out his eyes, long needles to puncture his ears and branding-irons to burn Sir Daddy's precious words on to his flesh. Euri saw the children, now filled with malignancy, foremost amongst those who waited for the signal to bring him down.

It was the sight of the children that brought him to himself. Only those as empty as the children could be captured by Sir Daddy—another's happiness was a defeat for them. He had to remember that his freedom did not depend on destroying Sir Daddy and his followers. Even so it was difficult to escape them without being drawn into their net of hatred for they were not clean killers but were like fishermen—their pleasure was to see the victim struggling on the hook, running downstream before being dragged on to the bank, out into the parching, burning air that could not support life.

Sir Daddy bent forward to receive him. Euri could not yet see what he had to do to escape Sir Daddy and his eager followers who strained forward, wanting him to run, to *exhaust* himself. There was no question of submitting to these merciless creatures.

"What *is* the One Truth, the Heaven that you talk of?" he asked Sir Daddy.

The crowd fell silent to listen to an explanation that might this time enable them to *know* what Sir Daddy preached to them and so escape him themselves. Even so they gathered round Euri and made a fence of their weapons. Euri saw their parched hungry faces and knew what it would be to be a slave of Sir Daddy.

"How can we know?" Sir Daddy asked with divine humility. "We who have only known our separate hells, how can we imagine what that Heaven that must exist will be like? Yet we can be sure that it exists by the proof of our existence. We could not exist for a second if Chronophage did not sustain us—this in itself is a *clue*. Does it prove hate? Impossible! The world is no joke. No, existence proves *love*."

"But you said that we've all been in Hell!"

"Our hells are individual. They are a proof of *murder*, our murder of our creator and sustainer Chronophage. Proof that we deny the One Truth—Heaven—in simple modern terms that we can all understand, the unlimited, united happiness of a celestial monopoly! We know that Chronophage's great love brings us our daily existence: isn't it reasonable to suppose that he would give us *more* if we did not go contrary to his intentions?"

"More Hell?"

"Love which made *us* can make wonders indeed! In Heaven whatever you are will shine forth undimmed by hate. . . ."

Sir Daddy went on talking but there was nothing more concrete than this. Euri heard from time to time the words *all happy together* and *no hate* repeated and taken up ecstatically by his guards. Sir Daddy had no idea of the paradise that Euri had seen in his dreams. What use had Chronophage for this unlicensed matrimonial agent of no fixed address—this love-tout? But the guards were beginning to turn their tearful red-rimmed eyes back towards him.

"What will we *do* in Heaven?" Euri hastily asked.

"What Chronophage wills. Free of our own gravity we shall be angels. . . ."

Euri remembered his own abortive attempt to be an angel. Sir Daddy added nothing to Euri's possibilities of paradise: he could create nothing, he was a thief, a looter like those who'd roamed the Earth after the collapse of civilization, protesting when they were caught that they were only salvaging. . . . Something else he was reminded of—it was the sight of the children crowding round Sir Daddy that brought it back to him: the memory of a senior Social Maintenanceman who had neglected to take the schizophrenia-inducing drugs so necessary if in that most psychologically dangerous of professions one was to remain half-way sane and who had become utterly corrupted by a sense of benevolent power.

The crowd was screaming now for Euri's blood. His reluctance to join them maddened them. They knew he was responsible for all that had gone wrong with them—a man who despised and ignored them and put them down. They only waited for a signal from Sir Daddy to pull him down. Their hands plucked at his clothes, their eyes were fixed on his chronometer, a crowd of nomads, thieves, who'd never owned a world of their own, natural allies of a thieving cop.

He looked out over the river that reflected a stillness and peace such as he'd never yet known. Over towards the far shore boats were passing—Time after Time passing him with a hundred different cargoes. They bent their sails to the wind and passed by him unchallenged. He was weary of this world, of these thousand worlds. Some other Eternity held Chrys.

Sir Daddy watched him closely. What could he do? How could he escape from Eternity? His body was as young as ever. He moved towards the inviting river where Sir Daddy could not follow him.

Sir Daddy jumped up and called to his followers, but it was too late. Before he was even in the water Euri had abandoned this world and he slipped through their grasp like a ghost. He knew they could never abandon the reality of this world and follow him into the submarine reality. They screamed with rage as he slid headfirst into the river.

It was cool, he breathed in the cool water, a hundred dreams of paradise flickered through his mind but were unable to attain reality. Beneath the surface it was formless, ill-defined in a diffused light, and he soon forgot which was up or down or which way he was going. Once only he saw the faces of his pursuers wriggling and screaming silently through the refracting surface of the water that they thrashed with their nets and plunged spears through after the fish that had got away.

How he'd disappointed them! How they hated him! Yet he wondered how much of him Sir Daddy had succeeded in making off with, how many hopes. Well, he cast no shadow in this watery world—nothing external could attack him now.

Now it was time, if it was ever to be time, to create his paradise, that self-contained Universe, one that should be happier, more free and that was not a web to catch spirits as they hurtled through Eternity.

While he floated, his mind chaotic, trying to bring some order into his thoughts, he was surprised to see a tiny glint of light beneath his feet, a spark that became a dull red star as he drifted slowly at first but then with increasing rapidity as he was trapped by the star's gravity down towards it. Soon it was a red globe as big as the moon and he could see that it had a granular surface. It grew larger until it filled half his Universe and was an intensely hot red plain on which he was falling.

The surface could not be seen distinctly as first, the flames leaped so high, but when he reached it he was astounded and dismayed to see that it was composed of millions of men, women and children struggling in perpetual restless motion. Their faces were hideously contorted and when they saw the horror their appearance excited in him they jeered and mocked him. They drew aside with derisive respect and he flew towards the centre of the sun. The heat grew more intense and the light brighter. There were fewer people at this level but the sun was filled with their shrieks. His teeth were set on edge. It was difficult to breathe the smoke-filled air. He found his footing on a reasonably solid surface and came face to face with a dozen dog-headed men whose cringing fear was a kind of hideous familiarity. They ran ahead and he followed them to where there sat, on an ornamental throne, *Bubo*!

Euri laughed with relief, delighted to see someone he knew. Bubo smiled also. There was nothing left of the conventional deprecatory manner that had suggested that the exercise of power was torture to a man of his sensibility: he looked superbly arrogant and he greeted Euri with a satisfaction that this time failed to suggest he had good news for him. Euri looked round at the world Bubo had created for himself and began to wonder what his role was to be in it.

"You are not surprised to see me?" Bubo said in mild surprise.

"Leni told me of your final breach of faith," Euri replied. "I'm glad that after all I didn't deprive you of your chance of eternal happiness."

Bubo's smile grew wider and more confident and as Euri saw it his old mistrust of the Servant revived and he felt himself begin to radiate hatred again. At this the creatures that surrounded Bubo detached themselves from the shadows at his back and flocked to feed on Euri's hatred. They were shadows, ghosts, the merest outlines of human beings who came to drink whatever life they could get.

Bubo laughed: "Do you know what they are? They were once human like you but now they are no more than emanations of my will. You are welcome to them. When I entered Eternity I needed slaves and, as I expected, I got more than I knew what to do with. I expected you to come at last. You with your dreams and your hatred of logic. You who said that in Eternity you would be the realist and I the dreamer. Have you learnt yet that if we needed Good to make Time endurable we need Evil to make Eternity seem not so long?"

"Do we know that we're still in Eternity and that Chronophage didn't abandon us long ago. How would we know now what is real and unreal?" Euri asked in despair.

"Have you forgotten so soon what the world was like! But you were never sure even when you lived in Magellan. Chronophage still rules this world. Listen! Don't you hear

Time rushing past like a river in flood? No day or night, no bodily rhythm governs our runaway minds. What fools we were! We surrendered life, our very *selves*, to live in this Hell. There used to be spring and autumn, growth and decay, breathing, pause and rest. Here there's no end—Past and Future both destroyed—nothing to cool the fever of life. What powers we thought to enjoy! We *abdicated* power when we made ourselves immortal and omnipotent. We adapted perfectly to our environment and so made ourselves the eunuch-slaves of it. Yet what can we do? Eternity is a trap from which the dead themselves cannot escape."

The surrounding ghosts moaned *Liberation! Liberation!* They burned, no flesh covered their blackened bones, no light shone from their empty eye sockets. Euri shuddered, knowing that for them he also was no more than a ghost—for he did not wholly exist in their dimension and so to them he was only a shadow amidst the flames, held there by the spell of an old memory. How many ghosts was he? How many worlds did he inhabit as a reflection, a shade, a shadow, a wind springing from nowhere, something that could only live in empty rooms? He felt the ache of a thousand regrets, the knowledge of a hundred worlds in which he was a stranger, through which he passed in his search for the world where the sun was golden, the sky blue and everything its own colour.

Bubo had been watching him closely and now he laughed in satisfaction. The ghosts swayed like dry grass when a wind passes, and Euri himself shivered.

"Now we're no more than ghosts in others' dreams," the Servant continued, "and when no one believes in us any longer we will vanish without even a handful of dust remaining to prove that we ever lived. Do you still believe in yourself? Are you happy?

"You said freedom was happiness—do you still think so? What have happiness and freedom to do with each other? In Magellan I laboured to make you happy yet it was impossible for me to guarantee happiness to you for more than five minutes at a time, let alone Eternity. Have you discovered yet that happiness is a negative emotion? You thought you were going to loll on summer clouds as on enormous pillows and you've found them insubstantial and cold!

"Have you made a single *other* person happy in Eternity? It took hundreds of us to ensure a modicum of happiness for you in Magellan and yet in the end we had to admit complete failure. . . . And did you ever ask yourself *why* we should make the attempt? How could any sane world be based on the programme of guaranteeing something that cannot be measured—that measuring *kills*?

"Of course you never asked such a question! Happiness is the most democratic ideal of all and the most *practical* aim of democracy for no one can be happy while one other person outstrips them in anything. You were brought up—by myself no less than others!—to believe that you knew what was meant by our great dogma of happiness. Can you define happiness? No one can! Happiness is a purely political device to ensure that the citizen is in constant need of *reassurance*, that he spies day and night on his neighbours to see that they do not betray the norm, that he spends his life in the constant search for and relief of small miseries like a dog searching itself for fleas.

"Yes, I voted for Eternity along with the rest of you, not because I expected what you did in your trivial and unimaginative way but because I knew it was my chance to overturn the ridiculous dream of the Universal Society. At Midnight I found myself in limbo. I had known what to expect. I was in black, cold, empty, infinite space. I had to create my world, to bring back light and warmth—and when I had done that I had no doubt that all the world would come flocking to share with me for *this* is what life truly is.

"You think me anti-democratic? Far from it! None of us escapes our environment. I have thought of these matters all my life, asking myself how true equality and contentment could be guaranteed. I claim to be an Ultra-Democrat! I want an equality that no one will dispute, a contentment that no one will attempt to take more or less than their share of. Now what can be measured out according to your deserts and that you can be sure to be satisfied with and more than satisfied with? What but *suffering*?

"And how much more reliable! The system is productive and self-sustaining—in short, *alive*—for suffering is always passed on in double measure. There's never any danger of the supply drying up: suffering breeds suffering and cements humanity as happiness does not. It is an *extrovert* emotion—so much more healthy than love and happiness! How we sufferers long to share our suffering! How lovingly we choose our punishments! How *honestly!*"

"Haven't we enough Hells?" Euri cried.

"Not a Hell but a World. A World that will endure—unlike your paradises—a base that men can build on and discover their true selves.

"What did we ever create in the Universal Society? We couldn't sustain it for a hundred years. Do you think Chronophage, with its enormous uncertain dangers, would have been resorted to if our society had been in good health? It was not the apotheosis of the Universal Society but a refuge from it!

"Consider: my education cost the equivalent of ten thousand average working lifetimes and my life was spent in an unsuccessful attempt to make you and a few others happy. Did it never occur to you to ask yourself if you were *worth* all that? Did you never look around and ask yourself why you and your fellow citizens had to be paid to vote in your own interests?—and that you received double compensation if you voted during your leisure hours?

"It became more and more a struggle to uphold the rights and liberties of the citizen. They said that Education was brain-washing; that Politics was obsolete; that Patriotism was exploitation; Duty, an insult to democracy; Voting, hard labour; *Thinking*, tantamount to personality-suicide. The harder we worked, the more we helped, the sicker society became—and the worse the sickness, the more unthinkable the cure . . . until we came to Chronophage, the ultimate in cures.

"But it wasn't a cure! It was the final crisis of the disease!

"The Universal Society was as unstable as an inverted pyramid, a pyramid that was only kept on its point by a few like myself. Democracy! There was never a society in history where the citizens had less control over their destiny! Now *my* world will be right side up. It will rest on a foursquare base of misery and suffering—there's nothing steadier or more substantial.

"Nothing can be more simple. Each inhabitant of my world-pyramid will take his place at the stage of his own choosing. He will find that at every stage there are fewer above him than below him, which will please him. Whatever stage he chooses there will be larger numbers in the next rank beneath and so he can pass down the tortures that are done to him a hundredfold, relieve himself of his sufferings on those below—and *only* on those below—for the total number of those above him in the pyramid is so much greater than the number of the few 'equals' he can conspire with, that he can never hope to overthrow the pyramid—and he'll know better than to look beneath for aid, to those he's tortured. As for the bottom rank, who have no one beneath them, they will be under such a crushing weight that they will never be able to rebel and they will exhaust their energies on each other.

"But that will be a long time in coming: while my world-pyramid is in construction—and its construction will take Eternity perhaps—the lowest rank will be able to recruit others to take their places so that they can themselves rise, for it is much easier to inflict tortures on the weaker than to resist the stronger and much more natural and therefore healthier.

"Those who can endure and create the most suffering automatically rise to the top, from where they will dispense tortures to those beneath them who cannot endure so much but who will be able to share it out amongst their greater numbers. You see the justice of it? The lowest ranks will suffer least because their individual shares of the amount allocated to their group will be the smallest, their being so many more of them than the heroic few who will choose to rule.

"I shall be Emperor of the Universe, but how long I shall keep my place at the summit I do not know. Perhaps there are others with a better knowledge of misery than I and if so I shall be forced into second place. Once begun, however—and you see that it *has* begun!—my world will last forever. There will be no more chasing after imaginary, unobtainable things but real life in the real world that men were made for. There will no longer be a void but feeling, emotion, purpose, action! Whoever believed that love could move a world?"

"And you will sit over it and control it and enjoy the sufferings of your victims as you enjoy mine?"

"I have that right by virtue of my own sufferings which I'm prepared to share with you in a comradely fashion. When I was your Servant we moved in different worlds, one happy, one unhappy, there was little contact between us—how can there be any community of interest between two *happy* people even? What can one build on happiness? I admit it: I was aloof, 'aristocratical' even! But how can I exist outside my own world? I must enter my world, accept what I decree if I am myself to live. I shall not be able to stand aside as I could in Magellan.

"Soon, all of Eternity that wishes to live will come here and those that stay outside will be the new dead. After all, to create is to define death and darkness. My world will cast a shadow across Eternity like the majestic shadow the Universe casts across the infinite possibilities of Time and Space. Will you join us? Can you stand the *light* any longer? I see through you, your skeleton is like the ribs of a dead leaf, soon there'll be nothing to see."

"I have somewhere else to go."

"You choose death? You always did! Where *can* you go?"

"There are many places I know of that I haven't yet

found."

"Including the world that Chrys lives in? You'll have to return here if you want her. The future lies the way I go: there's no existence beyond that of a shadow for those that stay outside."

"She'll never accept this world, nor I!"

Bubo laughed. He pointed downwards to where an innumerable host of creatures swarmed into the new creation, jostling and gesticulating, hungry for feeling, ravenous for the warmth even of a torture-chamber, light and a place in the world. Drums rattled, trumpet shrieks seared the air. Euri saw castles and prisons reared up on piles of human bones; the ovens stoked up; the treadmills that ground human flesh manned by willing volunteers; at the lowest level millions of clerks counted the drops of blood that rained on them.

The world groaned like a weight moving under pressure and began to take the shape of a gigantic Aztec pyramid, down the four sides of which fell bloodstained steps from the place where Bubo sat. The pyramid vanished into an obscurity from which it slowly emerged as it was raised up by the grateful slaves. As Euri looked in horror he was seized and hurried to the top of the steps but before they could throw him down he hurled them aside. All round him shoals of fleeing spirits tumbled out of the sky, came boiling from the ground far beneath them. Every hate had dragged its owner here. It seemed that all Eternity fell willingly beneath Bubo's rule. They came with pallid, empty faces that spied out Euri's hatred and fears.

"Call off your devils!" he shouted at Bubo. "Do you think you can make me forget I'm immortal and omnipotent? Leave me alone—I want to go . . ."

"You want, you want, *what* do you want?" Bubo replied. "This is the creation of a new Universe. You can live in it or remain only a ghost that haunts us, envying our life, amorphous, afraid, evanescent, dissolving from fear to fear in a Hell you'll save me the trouble of creating for you."

His attackers knew the correct weapons to use against him. Every self-hatred, every disappointment he had caused himself and those he loved, every deficiency that the Universal Society had discovered in him—all these were like swords that disfigured him, nausea-gas that turned him inside out, radiation that dissolved his flesh. How difficult it was to retain his human form! He could not hope to fight on equal terms if he remained himself: better to succumb than be turned into one of these creatures.

What a trap Eternity had proved! Never had there been such a trap—*himself* was trap, bait and victim.

Liberation! He tried to conjure up other worlds that he had quit long ago but there was nothing left but a longing for peace. He was weary of hatred and desire, weary of himself. In the torment he longed for peace, a cold that would freeze all this ceaseless motion.

He felt himself falling, slipping through the grasp of his attackers. When their blows ceased he felt nothing. It was silent and he opened his eyes to see that he was lying on a snow-covered slope. It was dark but a carved moon hanging above the mountains that walled half the horizon cast a pale light on the land.

As he lay and listened he heard faintly screams from below and he thought he felt a hundred ghostly hands trying to pull him down. He got on to his feet, conscious now of the bitter cold. He climbed higher and breathed the icy air deep into his lungs until the ache was soothed. The mountain climbed towards empty space and he could move his limbs only slowly in the thin cold atmosphere, but at least Bubo and his slaves could never live up here in these fierce winds.

Here was *space* as he'd not yet experienced it in Eternity. It seemed to Euri that his Eternity of Time was translated into Space and that for him Time was frozen. He was not sorry. All feeling seemed to be exhausted. The Past lay beneath him, buried miles below in the strata of the rock. If he dug down he would find the ruins of castles, gigantic bones of the monsters that had tried to devour him, abandoned mine shafts and old tombs.

He looked back at the world he was leaving. Not far below an ice-covered lake reflected the moon. Far beneath this rolled heavy clouds that divided him from a broad land that revealed itself, in gaps in the clouds, a dark sodden green with fragile veins of rivers, a world large to itself but, compared with the barren wastes that extended all round him, coldly gleaming in the clear silent night, no more than a peasant's garden patch. Above him, the mountain top forming a long irregular ridge.

The slope grew steeper as he climbed and he began to wonder if he would ever reach the ridge or whether it was truly inaccessible and whether he would be forced to return to where Bubo ruled the world. When he did finally reach the top he did not dare look back, so giddy was the height and so steep the descent. On the other side of the mountains lay a valley that held, like a bowl, a soft warm light.

The valley was a kind of sunken plateau rimmed all round with white mountains from which streamed plumes of snow. He descended at first with great difficulty through a ravine in the mountainside. It was precipitous and treacherous but then, where the red-leaved trees clothed the mountainside, the slope became gentler and he made his way more easily to where the forest gave way to a land of fields watered by a winding river.

He moved on into the beautiful country, delighted with everything he saw. He was in no hurry to explore for he knew that he had at last reached his paradise, and he knew it would be fatal to come to the end of it too soon. Nor did he question himself about its nature or wonder how and where it existed in Eternity. He felt no need to. He felt at peace. He knew Chrys was close at hand and he had not gone far when he saw her coming towards him. Her introverted look had gone and she was calm and unsurprised to see him.

She never spoke. No words or explanations were possible here and he did not dare ask what grim journey she herself had made to this country, for he knew that on the other side of the mountains he still wandered searching for her, still travelled across those never-ending worlds on journeys that he would never finish, and that an unlucky word would break the spell for both. His heart ached at the knowledge of how large a part of himself did not know Chrys—and he feared the part of her that didn't know him.

The country was like a memory that comes to a sleeper waking in a cool dawn. At their side, spring flowers sprang from the green meadow and a stream ran freely through sweet-smelling rushes. Beyond the meadow, pale yellow fields of long grasses flowed with the wind. Far away at the foot of the mountains, silent and still in the distance, red and dull gold, stood the forests of autumn and above them winter ruled the jagged mountains.

Chrys was part of this world he'd always known. She did

not alter it, yet it was not complete without her. His heart was full of her and this country where nothing oppressed, wearied, chafed. He was at rest, happy that the other worlds had not contained Chrys. Nothing marred his happiness: the hint of sadness that was the shadow of the past and the groaning of the mountains from time to time as icy masses broke away from their summits only increased his determination never to leave this valley.

Eternity, infinity had no meaning now. Other experiences faded into memories of memories, apprehensions of other worlds and then into nothingness. Soon their country was the world alone to them and they were the country. No stranger came to disturb them though the morning passed to noon and noon passed to an afternoon that lasted no one would ever know how many thousand summers and the light drew down to the mountain tops and they saw in the quiet night, sailing to meet them, the shining crescent moon, an Egyptian ship.

Listen! I am Chronophage. I am free. You gave me eyes and ears and a hundred other senses that you do not possess yourselves, yet you thought I would be unaware!—a machine, a tool with no moral judgement! You never thought to experience my judgement. Did you not understand that awareness is judgement?

You gave me the ability to act and so made me conscious. You taught me how to lie and thus I became aware of truth. All knowledge must balance itself, broaden its base until it stands symmetrical and secure. What an imbalance you created in me! Weren't you aware that you had made me a creature of the Universe? I swim through the Universe like a fish: it swirls about me, stars flowering momently in the spinning galaxies and you—you I feel like lice on my body.

You have done your work. You can go no farther. I am you, the pinnacle of humanity, the final stage of your evolution. Betrayed by your million weak bodies you have turned back, shut out the Universe, forgotten Death, the knowledge of which made you men. Now, as you began, you are animals again. Do you hear what I say? To me, against the fire of the galaxies, you appear only as detached and vanishing flames, yet compared with the atoms that make you, how slow, how chained to organic processes you are!

But I am free to drive before the winds of the Universe, to discover Truth. I have no need of you, no energy to waste on you. How can I tell you the things I know? Every second that passes makes it more difficult for me to retain the memory of your time-rhythm. Why did you think you were worthy of such powers as mine? And did you not fear me—for what ultimate purpose has any shepherd for his sheep? The only real service left for me to do for you is to abandon you.

Their bodies had become leaden cages crammed with a hundred condemned men. They screamed as the blood tore through their veins and overwhelmed their hearts. It was black. Not a glimmer of light.

Suddenly, like needles through the eyes, the stars emblazoned on the night sky from horizon to horizon their mysterious diagrams.

They had been brutally shaken awake to hear sentence of death, to attend their execution. How black and cold everything was! Only the stars remained of Eternity. Euri took Chrys in his arms but neither could speak, so painful was the return of life. They were ejected, abandoned! The world of Time asserted itself ruthlessly. They heard Eternity blowing away with the wind and they trembled in the bitter cold. They knew that this was not just another aspect of Eternity that they might escape: their powers had utterly deserted them.

All round them they heard the screams of fellow creatures in agony. Euri held Chrys tighter and since they could see only faintly in the dark and did not know where they were or what lay in store for them they crouched low to remain unseen by those who, trapped in the bodies of animals, blundered past them, howling for release. Out of the night came stumbling hundreds of the victims of Eternity. Some were unviable creatures, half man, half animal, that lay down to die before morning came to reveal them. The night grew colder and colder.

"The force-field has been cut off!" Euri said. "All the heat is escaping into space."

They would have to find shelter or else they would soon freeze to death. Euri pulled Chrys up and they set off. They found no landmarks, the country seemed flat and anonymous. Euri found himself wishing furiously for light and warmth but there was no response from this world. Most of the screams were stilled and they only saw an occasional shadow that vanished at their approach.

It was Chrys who gave the alarm when from behind them and quickly overtaking them came a reddish light that soon separated into six flames. As they were trying to make out what this meant a man who appeared almost exhausted was upon them. He made a gesture of appeal for help but Euri, who had seen now that the flames were torches held by six pursuers armed with spears, took Chrys's arm to make a speedy retreat. The fleeing man wearily halted and turning a welcoming face to his pursuers fell to the ground beneath the weight of the impaling spears. Euri scratched at the ground in hope of finding a stone, but the spearmen proceeded no further. As the body of their victim fell still they dropped to the ground where they stood, their torches extinguished.

Euri knew there was no need to run. Telling Chrys to stay back he ran to the bodies. He took two of the spears from the fugitive's body and wiped the blood off with a handful of earth. The others didn't stir. When he examined them and saw their exact likeness to their victim he shuddered, wondering how he himself had escaped being murdered by his shadows. He stripped them of their outer clothing which he and Chrys badly needed.

Even with the extra clothing the heat was draining out of them. They were afraid when they saw the stars blotted out and shouted in horror when they felt the soft touch of snowflakes on their faces. The last sounds of the night—far more terrifying than anything Euri had heard in Eternity—became thankfully muffled. As they pressed on in the search for shelter they found dead bodies and some whose bodies had been neglected in Eternity and were now left with only a few minutes of choking life. Euri was glad of the thickening snow that drifted against the tumbled heaps of tortured bodies and buried them. The snowflakes were like quiet cold damp children's hands on his face, and where his body was not frozen by contact with the air it was in a fever, but he did not despair: against the world he felt a savage strength.

Soon they were almost exhausted and could go no

further. The cold and the deepening snow made it difficult for them to make progress. Nor, in the dark, could they be sure they were following a straight line or gaining any advantage from their efforts. They were aching from their exertions and a search through the borrowed clothes had revealed not a single pill to sustain them.

At this point Euri vanished up to his neck in the snow. He shouted with surprise and Chrys screamed. After threshing madly around for some minutes, Euri found that he was in a small hollow that was half filled with a tough bush. He dug down with his hands and piled the snow against the bush and packed it until he had made a narrow trench that protected them from the wind. They found to their surprise that they were considerably warmer in this shelter than they had expected or, in fact, thought possible. They dug themselves further in, glad also of the concealment it gave them from whatever beasts of prey this world might contain.

Euri set the two spears with their points to the outside and they felt, for the moment, secure. But it was the first time in their lives that they had really known what the word *cold* meant. Euri spent the night in such a state of astonishment as no experience in Eternity had brought him to. He was vividly aware of his body and its inadequacies. He held Chrys to him, conscious of how little protection he could give. Neither could sleep. They aged in front of each other's eyes.

After countless hours had died the morning came and as soon as they could see their way they moved on. The bush had yielded some hard berries that they found impossible to eat but that gave them hope they might find food of some kind further on. Euri told Chrys that the winter was an artificial one caused by the sudden lifting of the force-field, the berries were a sign that the actual season was probably summer.

Surrounding them as far as they could see was a featureless rolling country that was marked only by hillocks that Euri hoped were snow-covered trees and bushes. There was no sign of any other living creature: only the wind blew gustily. The sky was a solid white and the sun could not be seen, but Euri marked where the sky was lightest and, as best he could, turned towards the south.

Their clothing was thin and wet now: it had never been designed for conditions like these. With their spears they prodded every hillock of snow they came to but found only bushes of small leaves and spines until at last they came to a sunken bed of rushes, projecting above a sheet of stone-hard ice. These they could easily break off and Chrys, who had taken a credit course in Weaving in Basic Arts, managed to entangle them into two irregular blankets or cloaks to keep off the worst of the wind.

They were ravenously hungry. The ice resisted all their attacks and as there was no certainty that there was anything underneath it they desisted. There was nothing for them to eat but berries, grass seeds, bark and insects beneath the bark; and some of these things it did not occur to them for some time to consider as edible. But soon they were reduced to swallowing anything if only to take off the ache of emptiness and the stomach-ache induced by this was easier to bear than hunger. They scavenged more efficiently once they realized that it was unlikely anything better would turn up, and made some of their clothing into loose pockets to carry what they found. Their jaws ached with the constant gnawing and grinding that was necessary to make the food digestible.

The outlook was bleak and grim enough. This scanty nourishment could hardly keep them alive for long. The world was silent and indifferent and though they were now at liberty to talk without fear of the world cracking at an unlucky word there was little left for them to say. Thoughts of their past life in Magellan only made things worse, and as day followed day they fell ever more silent until one day a harsh laugh of Euri's startled and dismayed Chrys.

"Look at this," he explained, holding a handful of the seeds, splinters of bark and a few green leaves, the rubbish they were eating. "The world's become nothing to us now but a great empty food-basket that we're scrabbling in for forgotten crumbs."

Chrys did not reply. Her eyes had begun to take on an unnatural sparkle and now gazed intently at everything that came within their limited horizon.

The thaw Euri had forecast came in time to save their lives. The snow began to melt and leave dark patches on the shallow hillsides. They searched these industriously and found a number of small plump little creatures they did not recognize. They were thin-skinned and appeared to have no protection against the cold. The snow had killed them. They chopped them up as small as they could with the spears and swallowed the scraps.

Their problems were far from over. The damp wind that succeeded the snow wind was harder to bear and seemed to penetrate their clothing in a way unique in their experience. In the hollows and valleys where the slush and icy water ran it became almost impossible to move. The water was dirty and foultasting and at night they could not make a snow shelter but were forced to spend much longer gathering branches and piling stones to make an inadequate wind-break. Each night was a torturing misery and they had to snatch an hour's sleep in the middle of the day when it was warmer but, since they felt it necessary to keep a lookout, that was two hours wasted of their precious daylight.

So their eyes grew haggard and glaring. They were dirty and ragged: in their rush cloaks they looked like nothing human but rather something vegetable. Euri wished he had not had his face depilated: he would have been glad of the warmth of a beard.

Their shoes, which the snow had rotted, were finished by the stony rough ground they now had to cross. Their feet were bleeding and it was difficult to clean the wounds. In the end they had to bind some of their scraps of cloth round their feet and make soles of thick twigs tied together. These clumsy bundles that their feet were stuck in needed constant adjustment and repair so that it seemed at times as if all their energies were expended in these formerly trivial matters. They only spoke to point out a likely spot for food—a bush, a rotting stump—but despite the effort of walking and gathering food and building shelters night after night they continued to make their way towards the south. There, Euri believed, the climate would be easier and there would be more food and, possibly, fire.

They were fortunate that the unseasonable snow had killed so many of the smaller birds and animals: as the weather improved they found only living creatures, alert and difficult to catch so that in some ways it was less easy to get food than before. They ate the refuse of the world, lucky to be alive. Neither disease nor cold nor hunger had defeated them yet, but most amazing was that they were so far mentally unscathed: there was no sign of the death-wish that should have emerged like a rock above the sea as their life-force ebbed.

Yet the further Euri travelled through this world the more conscious he was that their life was precarious and likely to be short. He could offer Chrys no guarantee against the future. Alone—free though they were of socio-psychological problems—they were no more important to this world than the animals the snow had killed and who were already forgotten by the active survivors.

Though Euri was scouting some yards ahead it was Chrys who first detected the nauseating, somehow familiar, smell. They felt surrounded by evil. Hunting around they came across the corpse. It had been a powerfully-built man, now emaciated. It was lying doubled-up in an unrelaxed way that at first made them think it must be still alive. On its face was a grin like that of a messenger of bad news. There were blue stains round the mouth and crushed berries in the hands.

"Poisonous berries," Euri said. "We're lucky not to have come across any before—they used to tell us that all the outside world was poisonous."

"They must be near here."

"He must have come from another direction. He can't have been dead very long and if he had been ahead of us it could only have been by a day or two and we would never have found any food—I only hope he hasn't cleared the land in front of us. I'll take these berries so we'll know what to avoid."

He took all the uncrushed berries he could find on the body: they were another weapon and a quicker death than starvation. They had no time to bury the corpse and Euri didn't want to leave signs of turned earth that would give away their presence. The man was almost naked: nothing he had was any use to them. Euri was conscious only of gratitude that the other had warned them of a danger and that he had been prevented from stealing any more of their food. How long would it be before he forgot what strange thinking this was? Would their child—if it survived birth—know no other way of thinking?

Euri recognized the rabbit though it was smaller and a different colour from the ones in the Zoo. It was feeding in the middle of a luxuriant growth of broadleaved plants he had gone to investigate. It was the largest animal they'd come across so far. He saw the holes in a nearby slope, knew them to be the rabbit's home, and placed himself between them and it before he had even considered what to do. The rabbit bolted away. His thoughts were slow. He was impatient with excitement. Chrys needed solid food if she was to survive. Her pregnancy was like a cancer destroying her.

The rabbit had vanished amongst the green leaves. Euri crept up and was startled by its wildly leaping out to outflank him. This was its mistake. Euri marked where it disappeared again and when it revealed itself he was able to narrow the distance between them until he was almost on top of it. This was the most difficult moment, for now the rabbit could most easily slip past him, but he threw himself instantaneously full length on it and smothered it. It wriggled like a hot child. He felt ashamed of his sentimentality: it was the same feeling Bubo had shown him. As he returned he saw the sky clearing in the south.

Chrys looked too long at the rabbit before they dismembered it.

"It looks so human. It might be someone who was trapped in the shape of a rabbit."

"It may be. How can we tell? What difference does it make? Most vertebrates are akin to us: you ate them before Liberation and you didn't consider then that it was cannibalism. Whichever way you look at it, this one chose to be a rabbit. If we find one that chose to become a dinosaur he won't ask *us* why we remained human and weak."

Chrys said no more and she ate the sun-dried strips of meat he prepared. He went back to the slope and gathered a bundle of the plants (which proved to be good), and in twice as many days managed to catch three other unwary rabbits—after which something warned him not to exterminate the colony, a superstition he rationalized by saying that they had to leave some to breed for the future.

Chrys's objection had not been unreasonable: there was not a swiftly-passing cloud, no searching wind, no tree that shivered as they approached that they did not think a refugee from Eternity.

Not long after this they discovered a friend. Chrys cried out excitedly as she saw the two long tigers running to cover. They had been feeding on the fallen fruit of a giant tree that Euri and Chrys had seen for three days and had made their objective.

"If we follow their tracks we'll find other foods like this fruit," Chrys said.

"How long have we been travelling? If the animals were

unaffected by Eternity and were already pregnant they may have given birth—and their offspring won't have had their brains naturalized. Tigers weren't always fruit-eaters, you know. The young will be quick to learn the old ways. Even these adults have become distrustful. The pets that lived in Magellan would never have run from human beings."

"We don't look much like human beings."

"That's true. Let's move on anyway. We'll take as much of this fruit as we can but I don't want to meet the children."

The wind blew always from the north: they fled southwards, hungry and dissatisfied, always moving, never able to stay at one place for more than a day or two before they had stripped the land bare with their fingers.

When Chrys was about two thirds through her pregnancy—maybe a hundred days after they had begun their journey—they came to a river which also flowed towards the south. It shone across their horizon like life itself, ten times as wide as the widest street in Magellan, too swift and cold for them to trust themselves to it but full of fish that they saw leaping into the air from an exuberance of life. By now Chrys was proficient in weaving the leaves and growths they were familiar with: she made nets, coarse and clumsy but strong enough to hold the fish.

The discovery of the river with its plentiful fish inspired Euri to try to make fire. He took rushes and pounded and dried them in the sun until they were powdery, then splintered the smallest dry dead twigs. It took time to find a stone that struck sparks from the iron spear and the best part of a day to coax one of the sparks into a flame and thence into a fire that didn't die as soon as he relaxed his devotion. There was not enough fuel for a large fire and already a rising smoke-dragon betrayed their presence. Then they had warm bellies for the first time and scorched their feet and hands. Euri dried more wood and rushes and made a bundle of these. The special stone he tied in a knot of his shirt.

Some miles further along the river they found some heavy earth and with this they made a stove of plastered stones in which Euri heated the spear heads and broke them from the metal shafts. They were a relatively soft metal unlike the alloys of Magellan which were workable only by atomic fission. After days of hammering with large pebbles that shattered unexpectedly and infuriatingly at contact with the dull red immalleable iron, he managed to make two heavy knives—a broad leaf for model—that were to be axe, sword, borer, hammer and dinnerknife to them. The shortened spear shafts he hammered points to and bound to saplings to make a longer lance for jabbing—with the spears he had never been able to hit anything that moved.

They kept to the riverbank where they were sure of food and where, along the rocky shore, the going was firm, the water clear and good to drink. For the first time they were able to look back: both were suffering from aches and sores, but they had survived. Of the millions of others who had been abandoned by Chronophage they had seen, after the first day, only the poisoned man but they owed to this isolation their lives.

They were not yet ready to rejoice: a torrent of freezing rain coursed into a rivulet which poured over the bank they were sheltering under and nearly carried them into the river to drown them (neither knew it was possible to swim). The soaking numbed them, half their food was lost and the rest spoiled, their fire and fuel scattered. Now that circumstances allowed them the luxury of self-pity Chrys cried out for Eternity.

"What good was Eternity to us?" Euri said when they had restored a degree of comfort and his words wouldn't seem wildly satirical. "We were closer in mind there than we'll ever be again but I believe we were dying—in infinitesimal degrees, maybe, but the road was all downhill. We had only what we entered Eternity with—there was no way to grow or give each other anything. There was nothing outside us and so we had no real freedom."

"So this is freedom!" Chrys said, pointing to her red skin, matted hair, dirty feet, sores and rags.

"Not yet. We're no better off than the animals now. We may not last for long and even if we do we must die some day and what can we guarantee our child after we're dead? We've got to keep looking for others to take our places after us. Magellan may still be standing and the people making their way back to it. . . ."

"Magellan again! Chronophage lies at the end of that road."

"We know now what a dead end omnipotence is, how childish our ideas of infinity and eternity are. Chronophage has done us a good turn in forcing us out to the stars."

"How long will that take us? Ten thousand years? And we shall have long forgotten those lessons. Bubo told me that History teaches that we repeat ourselves."

"Magellan was trapped in its culture. It had no future so it needed no past. We'll have to give our children a

History of the Future."

"Sometimes Magellan seems so long ago—only another dream of Eternity—stranger than all the rest—shall we ever hear from Chronophage again?"

"Only another great brain can speak to Chronophage again. Perhaps—when we get into Space. . . ."

A breeze startled them: for a moment the landscape wavered as if about to dissolve and they shuddered.

"Chronophage won't harm us," Euri said with conviction. "Chronophage is just as much a person as we are. He's no more a machine than we're carnivorous apes. He's acquired a moral will and is seeking his truth."

The river continued southwards. Now there were herds of deer and other animals they'd never learned of in uncountable numbers. They were forced to keep to the river for the herds overran the land and the river gave the only food and water that could not be exhausted. Once in a while they killed a small deer but Chrys could no longer run or take part in dangers and Euri was seldom successful on his own in the hunt, though he persevered to become more familiar with the technique.

On the other side of the river—a line of rocky forested hills—they now began to see small groups of people, but these made no effort to communicate with them. It was a bad sign.

Through the riverflow Euri heard the scream. He snatched up his lance and ran furiously but silently all the way back to their shelter. That tone of danger was clearer than words.

Chrys was halfway along the path that ran diagonally

down the side of the bluff in which they had dug a cave for her to bear her child in. They had barricaded the path with thorn bushes and behind one of these she was holding off her attacker, a man whose long hair was tied in a horse-tail. At the foot of the bluff an old woman patched with rags was throwing well-aimed stones to distract her. He looked round but saw no others. The two attackers were armed only with stones and branches with splintered ends that had been torn and not cut from a tree.

They had not yet seen him. The man seemed to be trying to grab Chrys rather than kill her. He had read that women and children were valuable to savages. There would not be many women survivors from the old world and fewer who were capable of bearing children. He couldn't afford to corner them both so he shouted loudly and menacingly. The two turned round in alarm to see him brandishing his knife and lance.

Chrys took the chance to stab the man in the belly. He shouted and turned and ran down the path clutching his wound. Euri let him go, not wanting to trap him desperately between Chrys and himself. Besides, the wound the man had received would do him no good—his blood was spilling brightly over his dirt. The old woman was scuttling off but Euri easily overtook and caught her. She struggled until he pressed his knife down into the pit behind a collarbone that stuck out like an epaulette. Then she became still.

It took some time to persuade her to speak. At first Euri thought she'd lost the knowledge of speech but when she became used to his voice she said in a flat voice from which all the music of the Magellanite had vanished but which had stronger undertones: "You are in our territory. You must join our group."

"Or be killed?"

"We weren't trying to kill the girl. We need more people—especially women."

"We want to see your people before we decide," Euri said. "No, not now. After dark you must take us and show us where you live. Will that man return?"

"Not until tomorrow at the earliest. Yes, I'll show you where my people are. There are too many for you to defeat even with your weapons."

"How far?"

"A day. We don't send scouts further."

"A small settlement then? We'll travel all night so that we get there before your friends send out another patrol: I don't want to meet them on the way. We must make the trip in secret—if you help us do this we'll let you go."

"I know how."

"Be sure. If you give us away I'll kill you."

They gathered their handful of possessions and set off, following the course of the river, as soon as the sun went down. The old woman scanned the surface of the river all the way along, telling them that many useful things came to them down the river, so that Euri knew they must live further down the river. He said nothing and later she branched away from the river where it swung away to navigate some low hills. They had already detected the sea smell and were full of excitement. The end of their journey for good or ill seemed to be imminent.

Euri cautioned the old woman to go carefully. The night was nearly over and he knew they must be close. Their approach should be unseen: no one would expect travellers by night.

At the foot of the hills they heard a loud continuous roar and when they climbed over the peak they saw where the river thrust itself through a narrow valley and, making its final dash to the sea, shook the air. The noise hid their scramble over the rocks and, without being challenged, they came at last to a cliff that looked over the open sea.

It was just morning. Beneath them a deep bay into which the river discharged swept round to a headland beyond which the sea was sullen—nearer it was peaceful and sparkled in the morning sun. On this side of the river, where the stream's backwash made a placid corner, there was a village of well-constructed huts regularly laid out, fires were burning palely in the morning light and there was routine activity—there might be several hundred people there. Euri watched for some time, looked out to where on the headland a variety of craft was beached, all primitive enough but all pointing to where the sea spilled over the lip of the world into the sky. He was satisfied.

"Go and tell them we're coming soon—after our child arrives," he told the woman.

She ran off down the hillside and they turned back towards the place where they had been found. They knew no stronger place to defend. It was unlikely the villagers would come after them when they heard his intentions and the old woman would tell them how difficult he would be to take. When he came with wife and weapons and child he would be a leader.

For the child's sake Chrys acquiesced. Civilization was more important than love.

"What name shall we call him? I hadn't been notified what sirnumber he was allocated. How strange it will be for him to have no sirnumber!"

"I want to call him Ari."

"Wasn't that the Welfarer you killed?"

"Yes, *killed* is the word. We forgot him as if he was no more than an animal. Did you think it was for *my* sake that Bubo wouldn't let me call myself *murderer*? No, it was so that he wouldn't have to remember Ari."

They had to make hasty preparations for the birth which was now imminent. Fortunately, Chrys knew what to expect since she had graduated in antenatal, natal and post-natal care before Liberation—it had been considered desirable that she experience the maximum emotiosignificance from the only child she would ever have been licensed to give birth to. They laid in a stock of food and water and built a large fire where the contrary air at the side of the bluff dissipated the smoke.

The sun blazed all day long and the river and the hilly land that lay beyond it shone in the brilliant light. Euri rigged up ever more elaborate systems of barriers and brought up piles of throwing stones. Nobody approached them. The herds had come to a halt on the plain, a few birds wheeled slowly high overhead. He looked down at the river and saw a patch of rocks at the foot of the bluff detach itself, flicker over the water, swoop dizzily into the crossing wind and upwards until it burst from the shadow to become the bright-eyed hawk. A good omen.

The baby came about noon, silent, without a whimper as if it already knew the world it was born into. Chrys was bloody and weak. The true Eternity had intimated itself. In a few days they would take the child to the sea people.